孔子学院总部/国家汉办推荐
Recommended by Confucius Institute Headquarters (Hanban)

SONG LYRICS IN PAINTINGS

许渊冲◎译
陈佩秋 等◎绘

中国出版集团
中译出版社

目录 CONTENTS

IX 海上心情
Unfailing Integrity

海上心情

“流光容易把人抛，红了樱桃，绿了芭蕉”（蒋捷）；“今宵酒醒何处？杨柳岸，晓风残月”（柳永）；“云破月来花弄影”（张先）；“无可奈何花落去，似曾相识燕归来”（晏殊）；“但愿人长久，千里共婵娟”（苏轼）；“曲终人不见，江上数峰青”（秦观）；“叶上初阳干宿雨，水面清圆，一一风荷举”（周邦彦）；“莫道不销魂，帘卷西风，人比黄花瘦”（李清照）；“三十功名尘与土，八千里路云和月”（岳飞）；“稻花香里说丰年，听取蛙声一片”（辛弃疾）……多少年来这些脍炙人口的词句一直在人们的口中吟诵，在人们的耳边回荡。

词作为一种音乐文学在宋代达到高峰，并与唐诗和元曲并称中国韵文史三绝。拥有300多年历史的宋代在5000年中华民族文明史上算不上太长，国力也远不如唐代强盛，然而宋代，特别是北宋时期，以汴京（现开封）和临安（现杭州）为代表的都市繁盛程度却在中国历史上留下了浓墨重彩的一笔。人们可以从张择端的《清明上河图》中略窥一二。伴随着经济的发展、社会的稳定以及标榜文治立国统治者的倡导，宋词在宋代一时兴盛至极。两宋词坛，各种流派、风格的词家辈出，涌现出以苏轼、辛弃疾、李清照、柳永、周邦彦、姜夔等为代表的一大批杰出词家，他们创作的许多流传千古的词作影响至今。值得庆幸的是，历经千年，300余位词家创作的20000余首宋词被保存了下来，惠泽后人。

2012年，上海清河文化传播有限公司曾与国家汉办、孔子学院总部以及中译出版社有限公司以《唐诗三百首》为底本，延请上海中国画院陈佩秋先生等18位画师创作了108幅绘画作品并由著名翻译家许渊冲教授译成英文，推出一诗一画、中英文对照的《画说唐诗》，广受好评。有感于此，今年，我们携手上海八号桥文化产业投资有限公司，以许渊冲教授出版的中英文对照《宋词三百首》为蓝本，再度邀集江、浙、沪三地30位著名画师，精心创作了117幅绘画作品对应诠释117首宋词，以《画说宋词》再次面世。我们希冀通过这种方式能为中华民族优秀文化走出国门、走向世界作出我们的一份贡献。

费滨海

二〇一四年十二月二十五日于上海

Unfailing Integrity

"Oh, time and tide will not wait for a man forlorn: with cherry red spring dies, when green banana sighs." (Jiang Jie) "Where shall I be found at daybreak from wine awake? Moored by a riverbank planted with willow trees beneath the waning moon and in the morning breeze." (Liu Yong) "The moon breaks through the clouds, with shadows flowers play." (Zhang Xian) "Deeply I sigh for the fallen flowers in vain; vaguely I seem to know the swallows come again." (Yan Shu) "So let us wish that man will live long as he can! Though miles apart, we'll share the beauty she displays." (Su Shi) "When her song ends, she is not seen, leaving, on the stream but peaks green." (Qin Guan) The rising sun has dried last night's raindrops on the lotus leaves, which, clear and round, dot water surface. One by one the lotus blooms stand up with ease and swing in morning breeze." (Zhou Bangyan) "Say not my soul is not consumed. Should the west wind uproll the curtain of my bower, you'll see a face thinner than yellow flower." (Li Qingzhao) "To dust is gone the fame achieved in thirty years; like cloud-veiled moon the thousand-mile Plain disappears." (Yue Fei) "The ricefields' sweet smell promises a bumper year; listen, how frogs' croaks please the ear!" (Xin Qiji)...Over the years, these classic lyrics have been intoned by millions of people, reverberating in their ears.

Ci, as a sort of musical literature, peaked in the Song Dynasty. Song lyrics, Tang Poetry and Qu are regarded as the three incomparable literary forms in Chinese verse. With a history of over 300 years, the Song Dynasty is not long at all considering the 5,000 years of Chinese civilization, and it was far behind the Tang Dynasty in national power. However, in the Song Dynasty, especially the Northern Song Dynasty, thriving metropolises such as Bianjing (now Kaifeng) and Linan (now Hangzhou) turned out to be one of the highlights of Chinese history, and are featured in *Along the River During the Qingming Festival* by Zhang Zeduan. With economic development, social stability as well as gubernatorial advocacy purporting to manage state affairs by civilians, Song lyrics enjoyed rapid flourishing development in the Song Dynasty when prominent ci composers, from various schools, with distinctive styles, came forth one after another; the works created by composers such as Su Shi, Xin Qiji, Li Qingzhao, Liu Yong, Zhou Bangyan and Jiang Kui remain influential today. Fortunately, even after thousands of years, over 20,000 Song lyrics by more than 300 ci composers are preserved, benefiting future generations.

In 2012, Shanghai Qinghe Culture and Communication Co., Ltd., Confucius Institute Headquarters, and China Translation and Publishing House invited 18 painters, including Chen Peiqiu, of Shanghai Chinese Painting Academy to illustrate *The Three Hundred Tang Poems with 108* paintings, and jointly published the Chinese-English Tang *Poetry in Paintings* translated by Professor Xu Yuanchong, a distinguished translator, which has since been critically acclaimed. Considering this, we are cooperating with Shanghai Bridge 8 Cultural Industry Investment Co., Ltd. this year, and have invited 30 famous painters from Jiangsu, Zhejiang and Shanghai to illustrate the Chinese-English *Three Hundred Song Lyrics* published by Professor Xu Yuanchong. With 117 elaborately created paintings correspondingly illustrating 117 Song lyrics, the Chinese-English *Song Lyrics in Paintings* is released. In this way, we hope to make our contribution to helping excellent Chinese culture travel abroad and play a significant role on the world stage.

Fei Binhai

Written in Shanghai on December 25, 2014

宋人曹冠詞意圖　甲午佳製

凤栖梧｜兰溪

曹冠

桂棹悠悠分浪稳。烟幂层峦，绿水连天远。
赢得锦囊诗句满，兴来豪饮挥金碗。

飞絮撩人花照眼。天阔风微，燕外晴丝卷。
翠竹谁家门可款，舣舟闲上斜阳岸。

Phoenix Perching on Plane Tree

The Orchid Stream

Cao Guan

The laurel boat cleaving the waves slowly goes by,
Mist veils peaks low and high,
Green water joins the far-off sky.
My pocket with verse and rhyme is filled up,
In high spirits I drink in my golden cup.

The willow down and flowers in flight tease my eye,
A soft breeze blows in the vast sky,
Through willow branches swallows fly.
Whose green bamboo invites me to the door?
I moor my boat at sunset and go to the shore.

◀ 凤栖梧　兰溪｜洪健 绘
Phoenix Perching on Plane Tree | Painter: Hong Jian

卜算子

曹组

松竹翠萝寒，迟日江山暮。幽径无人独自芳，
此恨凭谁诉。

似共梅花语，尚有寻芳侣。着意闻时不肯香，
香在无心处。

Song of Divination

Cao Zu

You are cold among pines, bamboos and vines.
When over the land the setting sun shines.
Alone you're fragrant on a lonely lane.
To whom of your loneliness can you complain?

With the mume blossoms you may speak,
Whom lovers of flowers might seek.
But you would not exude fragrance to please;
It can't be sought for as the breeze.

◄ 卜算子 | 鲍莺 绘
Song of Divination | Painter: Bao Ying

如梦令

曹组

门外绿阴千顷，两两黄鹂相应。睡起不胜情，
行到碧梧金井。人静，人静。风动一庭花影。

A Dreamlike Song

Cao Zu

Outdoors green shade spreads far and wide;
Golden orioles sing side by side.
They wake and sadden me,
I rise and go around the well under the plane tree.
What a tranquil day!
What a tranquil day!
When the breeze blows I see only one flower sway.

长相思

陈东甫

花深深，柳阴阴。度柳穿花觅信音，君心负妾心。

怨鸣琴，恨孤衾。钿誓钗盟何处寻，当初谁料今。

Everlasting Longing

Chen Dongfu

Flowers in bloom
And willows loom.
I pass through them to seek your letter fine,
But your heart belies mine.

My lute is dead,
Lonely my bed.
Where is the vow by my headdress and pin you've made?
Now the bygone days fade.

◀ 长相思 | 朱新昌 绘
Everlasting Longing | Painter: Zhu Xinchang

翠带涵花也高也

一冬晴意写花皆遣兴时在海上

仲真周花甲

金人捧露盘｜水仙花

高观国

梦湘云，吟湘月，吊湘灵。有谁见、罗袜尘生。凌波步弱，背人羞整六铢轻。娉娉嫋嫋，晕娇黄、玉色轻明。

香心静，波心冷，琴心怨，客心惊。怕佩解、却返瑶京。杯擎清露，醉春兰友与梅兄。苍烟万顷，断肠是、雪冷江清。

◀ **金人捧露盘 水仙花**｜陈佩秋 绘
The Golden Statue with Plate of Dew | Painter: Chen Peiqiu

The Golden Statue with Plate of Dew

The Daffodil

Gao Guanguo

Like Southern cloud in dream,
Singing of the Southern moon,
Who mourns for the fairy queen alone?
Who has seen on the stream
Her stainless silk socks white
Treading on waves with steps light?
Turning her back to strip off,
She's slender and tender for man to love.
She faints in charming yellow hue
Like a jade bright in view.

Her sweet heart is tranquil
Amid waves chill.
A lute complains,
Her heart feels pains.
I am afraid
Rid of her pendants of jade,
She would return to fairy bower.
Holding a cupful of clear dew,
She'd drink with orchid and mume flower.
Mist-veiled for miles and miles till out of view,
It breaks her dream
To see the snow-clad clear stream.

一剪梅　舟过吴江 | 张桂铭 绘 ▶
A Twig of Mume Blossoms | Painter: Zhang Guiming

紅了櫻桃綠了芭蕉
桂銘作

一剪梅｜舟过吴江

蒋捷

一片春愁待酒浇。江上舟摇，楼上帘招。秋娘渡与泰娘桥，风又飘飘，雨又萧萧。

何日归家洗客袍。银字笙调，心字香烧。流光容易把人抛，红了樱桃，绿了芭蕉。

A Twig of Mume Blossoms

My Boat Passing by Southern River

Jiang Jie

Can boundless grief be drowned in spring wine?
My boat tossed by waves high,
Streamers of wineshop fly.
The Farewell Ferry and the Beauty's Bridge would pine:
Wind blows from hour to hour;
Rain falls shower by shower.

When may I go home to wash my old robe outworn,
To play on silver lute
And burn the incense mute?
Oh, time and tide will not wait for a man forlorn:
With cherry red spring dies,
When green banana sighs.

卜算子 | 答施

乐婉

相思似海深，旧事如天远。泪滴千千万万行，
更使人、愁肠断。

要见无因见，了拚终难拚。若是前生未有缘，
待重结、来生缘。

Song of Divination

In Reply to Her Love

Le Wan

My love is deep as the sea high;
The past is far away as the sky.
The thousand streams of tears I shed
Make me heart-broken and half dead.

If I cannot see you again,
Why don’t we cut to kill my pain?
If we are fated not to be man and wife,
Let us be married in another life!

◀ 卜算子 答施 | 朱新昌 绘
Song of Divination | Painter: Zhu Xinchang

唯有漁竿
明月上瓜洲
甲午仲夏
於滬上西陽 健

月上瓜洲｜南徐多景楼作

张辑

江头又见新秋。几多愁。塞草连天何处、
是神州。

英雄恨，古今泪，水东流。唯有渔竿明月、
上瓜洲。

The Moon over Melon Islet

Zhang Ji

How much grief to see the autumn wind blows
By the riverside again!
Frontier grass skyward grows.
Where's the lost Central Plain?

Our heroes' tear on tear,
Though shed from year to year,
With the eastward-going river flows.
Only the moonshine
With my fishing line
On Melon Islet goes.

◀ 月上瓜洲　南徐多景楼作｜洪健 绘
The Moon over Melon Islet | Painter: Hong Jian

别来闲整钓鱼竿

酒泉子

潘阆

长忆西湖。尽日凭阑楼上望，三三两两钓鱼舟，岛屿正清秋。

笛声依约芦花里，白鸟成行忽惊起。别来闲整钓鱼竿，思入水云寒。

Fountain of Wine

Pan Lang

I still remember West Lake,
Where, leaning on the rails, I gazed without a break.
Oh fishing boats in twos and threes
And islets in clear autumn breeze.

Among flowering reeds faint flute-songs rose,
Startled white birds took flight in rows.
Since I left, I’ve repaired my fishing rod at leisure,
Thoughts of waves and clouds thrill me with pleasure.

◀ **酒泉子** | 丁筱芳 绘
Fountain of Wine | Painter: Ding Xiaofang

酒泉子

潘阆

长忆西山。灵隐寺前三竺后，冷泉亭上旧曾游，三伏似清秋。

白猿时见攀高树，长啸一声何处去。别来几向画图看，终是欠峰峦。

Fountain of Wine

Pan Lang

I still remember West Mountain:
Three bamboo groves in front, shady temple in rear.
I've visited the Pavilion of Cold Fountain,
Where summer's cool as autumn clear.

I've often seen white apes climb up high trees.
Where are they gone after long, long cry?
Can I find West Mountain in the picture, please?
The painted mountain has no real peaks high.

◀ **酒泉子**｜庞飞 绘
Fountain of Wine | Painter: Pang Fei

長憶觀潮滿郭人爭江上望來疑滄海盡成空萬面鼓聲中弄潮兒向濤頭立手
把紅旗旗不濕別來幾向夢中看夢覺尚心寒甲午春寫酒泉子意

酒泉子

潘阆

长忆观潮，满郭人争江上望。来疑沧海尽成空，万面鼓声中。

弄潮儿向涛头立，手把红旗旗不湿。别来几向梦中看，梦觉尚心寒。

Fountain of Wine

Pan Lang

I still remember watching tidal bore,
The town poured out on rivershore.
It seemed the sea had emptied all its water here,
And thousands of drums were beating far and near.

At the crest of huge billows the swimmers did stand,
Yet dry remained red flags they held in hand.
Come back, I saw in dreams the tide o'erflow the river,
Awake, I feel my heart with fear still shiver.

酒泉子｜乐震文 绘
Fountain of Wine | Painter: Le Zhenwen

對瀟瀟暮雨洒江天
柳永词意

八声甘州

柳永

对潇潇、暮雨洒江天，一番洗清秋。渐霜风凄紧，关河冷落，残照当楼。是处红衰翠减，苒苒物华休。唯有长江水，无语东流。

不忍登高临远，望故乡渺邈，归思难收。叹年来踪迹，何事苦淹留。想佳人、妆楼颙望，误几回、天际识归舟。争知我、倚阑干处，正恁凝愁。

◀ 八声甘州 | 张培成 绘
Eight Beats of Ganzhou Song | Painter: Zhang Peicheng

Eight Beats of Ganzhou Song

Liu Yong

Shower by shower
The evening rain besprinkles the sky
Over the river,
Washing cool the autumn air far and nigh.
Gradually frost falls and blows the wind so chill
That few people pass by the hill or rill.
In fading sunlight is drowned my bower.
Everywhere the red and the green wither away;
There's no more splendor of a sunny day.
Only the waves of River Long
Silently eastward flow along.

I cannot bear
To climb high and look far, for to gaze where
My native land is lost in mist so thick
Would make my lonely heart homesick.
I sigh over my rovings year by year.
Why should I hopelessly linger here?
From her bower my lady fair
Must gaze with longing eye.
How oft has she mistaken homebound sails
On the horizon from mine?
How could she know that I,
Leaning upon the rails,
With sorrow frozen on my face, for her I pine!

诉衷情近 | 陈翔 绘 ▶
Telling Innermost Feeling | Painter: Chen Xiang

诉衷情近

柳永

雨晴气爽，伫立江楼望处。澄明远水生光，重叠暮山耸翠。遥认断桥幽径，隐隐渔村，向晚孤烟起。

残阳里。脉脉朱阑静倚。黯然情绪，未饮先如醉。愁无际。暮云过了，秋光老尽，故人千里。竟日空凝睇。

Telling Innermost Feeling

Liu Yong

The air is fresh on a fine day after the rain,
I stand in a riverside tower and gaze.
Afar the water stretches clear and bright.
Green hills on hills tower in the twilight.
I find the broken bridge and quiet lane
In fisher's village veiled in haze,
At dusk I see lonely smoke rise.

Seeing the sun sink,
Silent I lean on railings red,
With sorrow fed,
I'm drunk before I drink.
Boundless is my grief cold,
Evening clouds pass before my eyes.
Autumn turns old.
My friends stay miles away;
In vain I gaze all the long day.

对酒当歌

蝶恋花

柳永

伫倚危楼风细细。望极春愁，黯黯生天际。
草色烟光残照里，无言谁会凭阑意。

拟把疏狂图一醉。对酒当歌，强乐还无味。
衣带渐宽终不悔，为伊消得人憔悴。

◀ **蝶恋花**｜丁筱芳 绘
Butterflies in Love with Flowers | Painter: Ding Xiaofang

Butterflies in Love with Flowers

Liu Yong

I lean alone on balcony in light, light breeze;
As far as the eye sees,
On the horizon dark parting grief grows unseen.
In fading sunlight rises smoke over grass green.
Who understands why mutely on the rails I lean?

I'd drown in wine my parting grief;
Chanting before the cup, strained mirth brings no relief.
I find my gown too large, but I will not regret;
It's worth while growing languid for my coquette.

楊柳岸曉風殘月
王雁畫柳永雨霖鈴詞意

雨霖铃

柳永

寒蝉凄切。对长亭晚，骤雨初歇。都门帐饮无绪，
留恋处、兰舟催发。执手相看泪眼，竟无语凝噎。
念去去、千里烟波，暮霭沉沉楚天阔。

多情自古伤离别，更那堪、冷落清秋节。今宵酒
醒何处，杨柳岸、晓风残月。此去经年，应是良辰、
好景虚设。便纵有、千种风情，更与何人说。

Bells Ringing in the Rain

Liu Yong

Cicadas chill
Drearily shrill.
We stand face to face in an evening hour
Before the pavilion, after a sudden shower.
Can we care for drinking before we part?
At the city gate
We are lingering late,
But the boat is waiting for me to depart.
Hand in hand we gaze at each other's tearful eyes
And burst into sobs with words congealed on our lips.
I'll go my way,
Far, far away.
On miles and miles of misty waves where sail ships,
And evening clouds hang low in boundless Southern skies.

Lovers would grieve at parting as of old.
How could I stand this clear autumn day so cold!
Where shall I be found at daybreak
From wine awake?
Moored by a riverbank planted with willow trees
Beneath the waning moon and in the morning breeze.
I'll be gone for a year.
In vain would good times and fine scenes appear.
However gallant I am on my part,
To whom can I lay bare my heart?

宋張先詞意何兮

画堂春

张先

外湖莲子长参差，霁山青处鸥飞。水天溶
漾画桡迟，人影鉴中移。

桃叶浅声双唱，杏红深色轻衣。小荷障面
避斜晖，分得翠阴归。

Spring in Painted Hall

Zhang Xian

The lotus blooms in outer lake grow high and low;
After the rain over green hills fly the gulls white.
The painted boats on rippling water slowly go;
Our shadows move on mirror bright.

Two maidens sing the song of peach leaf in voices low,
Clad in light clothes apricot-red.
They come back with green shadow fed.

◀ **画堂春** | 何曦 绘
Spring in Painted Hall | Painter: He Xi

诉衷情

张先

花前月下暂相逢。苦恨阻从容。何况酒醒梦断，花谢月朦胧。

花不尽，月无穷。两心同。此时愿作，杨柳千丝，绊惹春风。

Telling Innermost Feeling

Zhang Xian

Before flowers, beneath the moon, shortly we met
Only to part with bitter regret.
What's more, I wake from wine and dreams
To find fallen flowers and dim moonbeams.

Flowers will bloom again;
The moon will wax and wane.
Would our hearts be the same?
I'd turn the flame
Of my heart, string on string,
Into willow twigs to retain
The breeze of spring.

◀ 诉衷情 | 鲍莺 绘
Telling Innermost Feeling | Painter: Bao Ying

剪牡丹｜舟中闻双琵琶

张先

野绿连空，天青垂水，素色溶漾都净。柳径无人，堕絮飞无影。汀洲日落人归，修巾薄袂，撷香拾翠相竞。如解凌波，泊烟渚春暝。

彩绦朱索新整。宿绣屏、画船风定。金凤响双槽，弹出今古幽思谁省。玉盘大小乱珠迸。酒上妆面，花艳眉相并。重听。尽汉妃一曲，江空月静。

◀ 剪牡丹 舟中闻双琵琶｜徐默 绘
Peonies Cut Down | Painter: Xu Mo

Peonies Cut Down

Zhang Xian

The green plain extends far and wide,
The azure sky hangs over waterside.
The endless river flows with ripples purified.
On willowy lanes there's no man in sight;
The willow falls down without shadow in flight.
People come back, drowned in slanting sunlight.
Girt with long belt and dressed with thin sleeves,
Girls vie in plucking flowers and green leaves.
They know how to tread on the waves, it seems,
On misty rivershore spring dreams,

Newly adorned with tassels red and ribbons green,
They live behind embroidered screen.
The painted boat goes without breeze.
The golden phoenix on the pipa sings with ease.
Who knows if the woe old or new is played?
Big and small pearls run riot on the plate of jade.
Flowers and eyebrows vie in beauty in vain.
Listen again!
When the princess sings of her dream,
It will calm down the moon and the stream.

天仙子

张先

时为嘉禾小倅，以病眠，不赴府会。

水调数声持酒听。午醉醒来愁未醒。送春春去几时回，临晚镜。伤流景。往事后期空记省。

沙上并禽池上暝。云破月来花弄影。重重帘幕密遮灯，风不定。人初静。明日落红应满径。

Song of the Immortal

Zhang Xian

Wine cup in hand, I listen to Water Melody;
Awake from wine at noon, but not from melancholy.
When will spring come back now it is going away?
In the mirror, alas!
I see happy time pass.
In vain may I recall the old days gone for aye.

Night falls on poolside sand where pairs of lovebirds stay;
The moon breaks through the clouds, with shadows flowers play.
Lamplights veiled by screen on screen can't be seen.
The fickle wind still blows;
The night so silent grows.
Tomorrow fallen reds should cover the pathway.

一曲新詞酒一杯去年天氣舊亭台夕陽西下幾時回無可奈何花落去似曾相識燕歸來小園香徑獨徘徊
浣溪沙 晏殊詞意
戴敦邦

浣溪沙

晏殊

一曲新词酒一杯，去年天气旧亭台。夕阳
西下几时回。

无可奈何花落去，似曾相识燕归来。小园
香径独徘徊。

Silk-Washing Stream

Yan Shu

A song filled with new words, a cup filled with old wine,
The bower is last year's, the weather is as fine.
Will last year reappear as the sun on decline?

Deeply I sigh for the fallen flowers in vain;
Vaguely I seem to know the swallows come again.
In fragrant garden path alone I still remain.

◀ 浣溪沙 | 戴敦邦 绘
Silk-Washing Stream | Painter: Dai Dunbang

离亭燕

张昇

一带江山如画，风物向秋潇洒。水浸碧天何处断，霁色冷光相射。蓼屿荻花洲，隐映竹篱茅舍。

天际客帆高挂，门外酒旗低迓。多少六朝兴废事，尽入渔樵闲话。怅望倚危栏，红日无言西下。

◀ 离亭燕 | 朱敏 绘
Swallows Leaving Pavilion | Painter: Zhu Min

Swallows Leaving Pavilion

Zhang Bian

So picturesque the land by riverside,
In autumn tints the scenery is purified.
Without a break green waves merge into azure sky,
The sunbeams after rain take chilly dye.
Bamboo fence dimly seen amid the reeds
And thatch-roofed cottages overgrown with weeds.

Among white clouds are lost white sails,
And where smoke coils up slow,
There wineshop streamers hang low.
How many of the fisherman's and woodman's tales
Are told about the Six Dynasties' fall and rise!
Saddened, I lean upon the tower's rails,
Mutely the sun turns cold and sinks in western skies.

木兰花 | 林曦明 绘 ▶
Magnolia Flowers | Painter: Lin Ximing

宋人词意图
甲午之夏林曦明

木兰花

宋祁

东城渐觉风光好。縠皱波纹迎客棹。绿杨烟外晓寒轻，红杏枝头春意闹。

浮生长恨欢娱少。肯爱千金轻一笑。为君持酒劝斜阳，且向花间留晚照。

Magnolia Flowers

Song Qi

The scenery is getting fine east of the town;
The rippling water greets boats rowing up and down.
Beyond green willows morning chill is growing mild;
On pink apricot branches spring is running wild.

In our floating life scarce are pleasures we seek after.
How can we value gold above a hearty laughter?
I raise wine cup to ask the slanting sun to stay
And leave among the flowers its departing ray.

甲午初夏於金陵喻慧畫

浪淘沙

欧阳修

把酒祝东风，且共从容。垂杨紫陌洛城东。总是当时携手处，游遍芳丛。

聚散苦匆匆，此恨无穷。今年花胜去年红。可惜明年花更好，知与谁同。

Sand-Sifting Waves

Ouyang Xiu

Wine cup in hand, I drink to the eastern breeze:
Let us enjoy with ease!
On the violet pathways
Green with willows east of the capital,
We used to stroll hand in hand in bygone days,
Rambling past flower shrubs one and all.

In haste to meet and part
Would ever break the heart.
Flowers this year
Redder than last appear.
Next year more beautiful they'll be.
But who will enjoy them with me?

欧阳修采桑子意早春
秦文聚若林居

采桑子

欧阳修

轻舟短棹西湖好，绿水逶迤。芳草长堤。
隐隐笙歌处处随。

无风水面琉璃滑，不觉船移。微动涟漪。
惊起沙禽掠岸飞。

Gathering Mulberry Leaves

Ouyang Xiu

Viewed from a light boat with short oars, West Lake is fair.
Green water winds along
The banks overgrown with sweet grass; here and there
Faintly we hear a flute song.

The water surface is smooth like glass when no wind blows;
I feel the boat moves no more.
Leaving ripples behind, it goes,
The startled waterbirds skim the flat sandy shore.

◀ 采桑子 | 乐震文 绘
Gathering Mulberry Leaves | Painter: Le Zhenwen

笙歌散盡遊人去始覺春空垂下簾櫳雙燕歸來細雨中歐陽修采桑子
群芳過後西湖好狼籍殘紅飛絮濛濛垂柳闌干盡日風

采桑子

欧阳修

群芳过后西湖好，狼藉残红。飞絮濛濛。
垂柳阑干尽日风。

笙歌散尽游人去，始觉春空。垂下帘栊。
双燕归来细雨中。

Gathering Mulberry Leaves

Ouyang Xiu

All flowers have passed away, West Lake is quiet;
The fallen blooms run riot.
Catkins from willow trees
Beyond the railings fly all day, fluffy in breeze.

Flute songs no longer sung and sightseers gone,
I begin to feel spring alone.
Lowering the blinds in vain,
I see a pair of swallows come back in the rain.

◀ 采桑子 | 萧海春 绘
Gathering Mulberry Leaves | Painter: Xiao Haichun

蝶恋花

欧阳修

庭院深深深几许。杨柳堆烟，帘幕无重数。
玉勒雕鞍游冶处，楼高不见章台路。

雨横风狂三月暮。门掩黄昏，无计留春住。
泪眼问花花不语，乱红飞过秋千去。

Butterflies in Love with Flowers

Ouyang Xiu

Deep, deep the courtyard where he is, so deep
It's veiled by smokelike willows heap on heap,
By curtain on curtain and screen on screen.
Leaving his saddle and bridle, there he has been
Merry-making. From my tower his trace can't be seen.

The third moon now, the wind and rain are raging late;
At dusk I bar the gate,
But I can't bar in spring.
My tearful eyes ask flowers, but they fail to bring
An answer, I see red blooms fly over the swing.

◀ **蝶恋花**｜陈向迅 绘
Butterflies in Love with Flowers | Painter: Chen Xiangxun

浪淘沙

王安石

伊吕两衰翁。历遍穷通。一为钓叟一耕佣。
若使当时身不遇，老了英雄。

汤武偶相逢。风虎云龙。兴王只在笑谈中。
直至如今千载后，谁与争功。

Sand-Sifting Waves

Wang Anshi

The two prime ministers, while young, were poor;
They had been fisherman and peasant before.
Had they not met their sovereigns wise,
In vain would they grow old. How could they rise?

When they had met discerning eyes,
The tiger would raise the wind the dragon the cloud.
They helped two emperors in laughter.
Now, in a thousand years after,
Who could rival them and be proud?

◀ 浪淘沙｜朱新昌 绘
Sand-Sifting Waves | Painter: Zhu Xinchang

王安石渔家傲
词意图
甲午

渔家傲

王安石

平岸小桥千嶂抱。柔蓝一水萦花草。茅屋数间窗窈窕。尘不到。时时自有春风扫。

午枕觉来闻语鸟。欹眠似听朝鸡早。忽忆故人今总老。贪梦好。茫然忘了邯郸道。

Pride of Fishermen

Wang Anshi

Surrounded by peaks, a bridge flies from shore to shore;
A soft blue stream flows through flowers before the door.
A few thatched houses with windows I adore.
There comes no dust,
The place is swept by vernal breeze in fitful gusts.

I hear birds twitter when awake from nap at noon;
I wonder in my bed why the cock crows so soon.
Thinking of my friends who have all grown old,
Why indulge in a dream of gold?
Do not forget the way to glory is rough and cold!

◀ 渔家傲 | 乐震文 绘
Pride of Fishermen | Painter: Le Zhenwen

春晓
甲午夏日健製於滬上

清平乐｜春晚

王安国

留春不住。费尽莺儿语。满地残红宫锦污，昨夜南园风雨。

小怜初上琵琶。晓来思绕天涯。不肯画堂朱户，春风自在杨花。

Pure Serene Music

Late Spring

Wang Anguo

Spring cannot be retained,
Though orioles have exhausted their song.
The ground is strewn with fallen reds like brocade stained,
The southern garden washed by rain all the night long.

For the first time the songstress plucks the pipa string;
At dawn her yearning soars into the sky.
The painted hall with crimson door's no place for spring;
The vernal breeze with willow down wafts high.

◀ 清平乐　春晚｜洪健 绘
Pure Serene Music | Painter: Hong Jian

我住長江頭君住長江尾日日思君不見君共飲長江水

卜算子

李之仪

我住长江头，君住长江尾。日日思君不见君，
共饮长江水。

此水几时休，此恨何时已。只愿君心似我心，
定不负相思意。

Song of Divination

Li Zhiyi

I live upstream and you downstream.
From night to night of you I dream.
Unlike the stream you're not in view,
Though we both drink from River Blue.

Where will the water no more flow?
When will my grief no longer grow?
I wish your heart would be like mine,
Then not in vain for you I pine.

◀ 卜算子 | 丁筱芳 绘
Song of Divination | Painter: Ding Xiaofang

蝶恋花

苏轼

花褪残红青杏小。燕子飞时，绿水人家绕。枝上柳绵吹又少。天涯何处无芳草。

墙里秋千墙外道。墙外行人，墙里佳人笑。笑渐不闻声渐悄。多情却被无情恼。

Butterflies in Love with Flowers

Su Shi

Red flowers fade, green apricots appear still small,
When swallows pass
Over blue water that surrounds the garden wall.
Most willow catkins have been blown away, alas!
But there is no place where grows no sweet grass.

Without the wall there is a path, within a swing.
A passer-by
Hears a fair maiden's laughter in the garden ring.
The ringing laughter fades to silence by and by;
For the enchantress the enchanted can only sigh.

◀ **蝶恋花** | 朱新昌 绘
Butterflies in Love with Flowers | Painter: Zhu Xinchang

料峭春風吹酒醒微冷山頭斜照卻相迎回首蕭瑟處也無風雨也無晴
東坡定風波詞意

定风波

苏轼

三月七日，沙湖道中遇雨。雨具先去，同行皆狼狈，余独不觉。已而遂晴，故作此词。

莫听穿林打叶声，何妨吟啸且徐行。竹杖芒鞋轻胜马，谁怕？一蓑烟雨任平生。

料峭春风吹酒醒，微冷。山头斜照却相迎。回首向来萧瑟处，归去，也无风雨也无晴。

◀ 定风波｜庞飞 绘
Calming the Waves | Painter: Pang Fei

Calming the Waves

Su Shi

Listen not to the rain beating against the trees.
Why don't you slowly walk and chant at ease?
Better than saddled horse I like sandals and cane.
O I would fain
Spend a straw-cloaked life in mist and rain.

Drunken, I'm sobered by vernal wind shrill
And rather chill.
In front I see the slanting sun atop the hill;
Turning my head, I see the dreary beaten track.
Let me go back!
Impervious to wind, rain or shine, I'll have my will.

江城子　孤山竹阁送述古 | 汪家芳 绘 ▶
Riverside Town | Painter: Wang Jiafang

蘇軾江城子 孤山竹閣送述古
翠蛾羞黛怯人看掩霜紈淚偷彈且盡一尊收淚唱
陽關漫道帝城天樣遠天易見見君難畫堂新構近孤山曲欄
干為誰安飛絮落花春色屬明年欲棹小舟尋舊事無處問水連天

江城子｜孤山竹阁送述古

苏轼

翠蛾羞黛怯人看。掩霜纨，泪偷弹。且尽一尊，
收泪唱阳关。漫道帝城天样远，天易见，见君难。

画堂新构近孤山。曲栏干，为谁安。飞絮落花，
春色属明年。欲棹小舟寻旧事，无处问，水连天。

Riverside Town

Farewell to Governor Chen at Bamboo Pavilion on Lonely Hill

Su Shi

Her eyebrows penciled dark, she feels shy to be seen.
Hidden behind a silken fan so green,
Stealthily she sheds tear on tear.
Let me drink farewell to you and hear
Her sing, with tears wiped away, her song of adieu.
Do not say the imperial town is as far as the sky.
It is easier to see the sun high
Than to meet you.

The newly built painted hall to Lonely Hill is near.
For whom is made
The winding balustrade?
Falling flowers and willow down fly;
Spring belongs to next year.
I try to row a boat to find the things gone by.
O whom can I ask? In my eye
I only see water one with the sky.

苏轼江城子词意图2014年夏

江城子｜密州出猎

苏轼

老夫聊发少年狂。左牵黄，右擎苍。锦帽貂裘，千骑卷平冈。为报倾城随太守，亲射虎，看孙郎。

酒酣胸胆尚开张。鬓微霜，又何妨。持节云中，何日遣冯唐。会挽雕弓如满月，西北望，射天狼。

◀ 江城子　密州出猎｜施大畏 绘
Riverside Town | Painter: Shi Dawei

Riverside Town

Hunting at Mizhou

Su Shi

Rejuvenated, I my fiery zeal display;
On left hand leash, a yellow hound,
On right hand wrist, a falcon grey.
A thousand silk-capped, sable-coated horsemen sweep
Across the rising ground
And hillocks steep.
Townspeople pour out of the city gate
To watch the tiger-hunting magistrate.

Heart gladdened with strong wine, who cares
About a few new-frosted hairs?
When will the court imperial send
An envoy to recall the exile? Then I'll bend
My bow like a full moon, and aiming northwest, I
Will shoot down the fierce Wolf from the sky.

东坡临江仙夜归临皋词意
培成画

临江仙｜夜归临皋

苏轼

夜饮东坡醒复醉，归来仿佛三更。家童鼻息已雷鸣。
敲门都不应，倚杖听江声。

长恨此身非我有，何时忘却营营。夜阑风静縠纹平。
小舟从此逝，江海寄余生。

Riverside Daffodils

Su Shi

Drinking at Eastern Slope by night,
I sober, then get drunk again.
When I come back, it's near midnight,
I hear the thunder of my houseboy's snore;
I knock but no one answers the door.
What can I do but, leaning on my cane,
Listen to the river's refrain?

I long regret I am not master of my own.
When can I ignore the hums of up and down?
In the still night the soft winds quiver
On ripples of the river.
From now on I would vanish with my little boat;
For the rest of my life on the sea I would float.

踏散芳英落酒卮
甲午 健

南乡子｜梅花词和杨元素

苏轼

寒雀满疏篱。争抱寒柯看玉蕤。忽见客来花下坐，
惊飞。踏散芳英落酒卮。

痛饮又能诗。坐客无毡醉不知。花尽酒阑春到也，
离离。一点微酸已著枝。

Song of the Southern Country

Mume Blossoms for Yang Yuansu

Su Shi

On the fence perch birds feeling cold,
To view the blooms of jade they dispute for branch old.
Seeing a guest sit under flowers, they fly up
And scatter petals over his wine cup.

Writing verses and drinking wine,
The guest knows not he's not sitting on felt fine.
Wine cup dried up, spring comes with fallen flower.
Leave here! The branch has felt a little sour.

◀ 南乡子 梅花词和杨元素｜洪健 绘
Song of the Southern Country | Painter: Hong Jian

南乡子

苏轼

怅望送春杯。渐老逢春能几回。花满楚城愁远别，
伤怀。何况清丝急管催。

吟断望乡台。万里归心独上来。景物登临闲始见，
徘徊。一寸相思一寸灰。

Song of the Southern Country

Su Shi

Wine cup in hand, I see spring off in vain.
How many times can I, grown old, see spring again?
The town in bloom, I'm grieved to be far, far away.
Can I be gay?
The pipes and strings do hasten spring not to delay.

I croon and gaze from Homesick Terrace high;
Coming for miles and miles, alone I mount and sigh.
Things can be best enjoyed in a leisurely way;
For long I stay,
And inch by inch my heart burns into ashes grey.

◀ 南乡子 | 朱新昌 绘
Song of the Southern Country | Painter: Zhu Xinchang

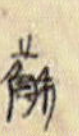

蘇軾圖

满庭芳

苏轼

蜗角虚名，蝇头微利，算来著甚干忙。事皆前定，
谁弱又谁强。且趁闲身未老，尽放我、些子疏狂。
百年里，浑教是醉，三万六千场。

思量。能几许，忧愁风雨，一半相妨。又何须、
抵死说短论长。幸对清风皓月，苔茵展、云幕高张。
江南好，千盅美酒，一曲满庭芳。

◀ **满庭芳**｜卢甫圣 绘
Courtyard Full of Fragrance | Painter: Lu Fusheng

Courtyard Full of Fragrance

Su Shi

For fame as vain as a snail's horn
And profit as slight as a fly's head,
Should I be busy and forlorn?
Fate rules for long,
Who is weak? Who is strong?
Not yet grown old and having leisure,
Let me be free to enjoy pleasure!
Could I be drunk in a hundred years,
Thirty-six hundred times without shedding tears?

Think how long life can last,
Though sad and harmful storms I've passed.
Why should I waste my breath
Until my death,
To say the short and long
Or right and wrong?
I am happy to enjoy clear breeze and the moon bright,
Green grass outspread
And a canopy of cloud white.
The Southern shore is fine
With a thousand cups of wine
And the courtyard fragrant with song.

亂石穿空驚濤拍岸捲起
千堆雪江山如畫一時多少
豪傑 金陵高雲畫赤壁
懷古於甲午年六月臥雲居

念奴娇 | 赤壁怀古

苏轼

大江东去，浪淘尽、千古风流人物。故垒西边，
人道是、三国周郎赤壁。乱石穿空，惊涛拍岸，
卷起千堆雪。江山如画，一时多少豪杰！

遥想公瑾当年，小乔初嫁了，雄姿英发。羽扇纶巾，
谈笑间、樯橹灰飞烟灭。故国神游，多情应笑我，
早生华发。人生如梦，一樽还酹江月！

Charm of a Maiden Singer

Su Shi

The endless river eastward flows;
With its huge waves are gone all those
Gallant heroes of bygone years.
West of the ancient fortress appears
Red Cliff where General Zhou won his early fame
When the Three Kingdoms were in flame.
Rocks tower in the air and waves beat on the shore,
Rolling up a thousand heaps of snow.
To match the land so fair, how many heroes of yore
Had made great show!

I fancy General Zhou at the height
Of his success, with a plume fan in hand,
In a silk hood, so brave and bright,
Laughing and jesting with his bride so fair,
While enemy ships were destroyed as planned
Like castles in the air.
Should their souls revisit this land,
Sentimental, his bride would laugh to say:
Younger than they, I have my hair turned grey.
Life is but like a dream.
O moon, I drink to you who have seen them on the stream.

牛衣古柳卖黄瓜
东坡词意

浣溪沙

苏轼

簌簌衣巾落枣花，村南村北响缲车。牛衣古柳卖黄瓜。

酒困路长唯欲睡，日高人渴漫思茶。敲门试问野人家。

Silk-Washing Stream

Su Shi

Date flowers fall in showers on my hooded head;
At both ends of the village wheels are spinning thread;
A straw-cloaked man sells cucumbers beneath a willow tree.

Wine-drowsy when the road is long, I yearn for bed;
Throat parched when the sun is high, I long for tea.
I knock at a farmer's door to see what he'll treat me.

◀ 浣溪沙 | 张培成 绘
Silk-Washing Stream | Painter: Zhang Peicheng

水调歌头

苏轼

丙辰中秋，欢饮达旦，大醉。作此篇，兼怀子由。

明月几时有，把酒问青天。不知天上宫阙，今夕是何年。我欲乘风归去，又恐琼楼玉宇，高处不胜寒。起舞弄清影，何似在人间。

转朱阁，低绮户，照无眠。不应有恨，何事长向别时圆。人有悲欢离合，月有阴晴圆缺，此事古难全。但愿人长久，千里共婵娟。

◀ **水调歌头**｜何曦 绘
Prelude to Water Melody | Painter: He Xi

Prelude to Water Melody

Su Shi

How long will the full moon appear?
Wine cup in hand, I ask the sky.
I do not know what time of year
'T would be tonight in the palace on high.
Riding the wind, there I would fly,
Yet I'm afraid the crystalline palace would be
Too high and cold for me.
I rise and dance, with my shadow I play.
On high as on earth, would it be as gay?

The moon goes round the mansions red
Through gauze-draped windows to shed
Her light upon the sleepless bed.
Against man she should have no spite.
Why then when people part, is she oft full and bright?
Men have sorrow and joy; they part or meet again;
The moon is bright or dim and she may wax or wane.
There has been nothing perfect since the olden days.
So let us wish that man
Will live long as he can!
Thousand miles apart, we'll share the beauty she displays.

行香子

苏轼

清夜无尘，月色如银。酒斟时、须满十分。浮名浮利，虚苦劳神。叹隙中驹，石中火，梦中身。

虽抱文章，开口谁亲。且陶陶、乐尽天真。几时归去，作个闲人。对一张琴，一壶酒，一溪云。

Song of Incense

Su Shi

Stainless is the clear night;
The moon is silver bright.
Fill my wine cup
Till it brims up!
Why toil with pain
For wealth and fame in vain?
Time flies as a steed white
Passes a gap in flight.
Like a spark in the dark
Or a dream of moonbeam.

Though I can write,
Who thinks I'm right?
Why not enjoy
Like a mere boy?
So I would be
A man carefree.
I would be mute before my lute;
It would be fine in face of wine;
I would be proud to cleave the cloud.

浣溪沙

苏轼

游蕲水清泉寺，寺临兰溪，溪水西流。

山下兰芽短浸溪，松间沙路净无泥。萧萧暮雨子规啼。

谁道人生无再少，门前流水尚能西。休将白发唱黄鸡。

Silk-Washing Stream

Su Shi

In the stream below the hill there drowns the orchid bud;
On sandy path between pine trees you see no mud.
Shower by shower falls the rain while cuckoos sing.

Who says an old man can't return unto his spring?
Before Clear Fountain's Temple water still flows west.
Why can't the cock still crow though with a snow-white crest?

◀ 浣溪沙 | 朱敏 绘
Silk-Washing Stream | Painter: Zhu Min

黄州中秋
甲午秋健

西江月 | 黄州中秋

苏轼

世事一场大梦，人生几度秋凉。夜来风叶已鸣廊，
看取眉头鬓上。

酒贱常愁客少，月明多被云妨。中秋谁与共孤光，
把盏凄然北望。

The Moon over the West River

Su Shi

Like dreams pass world affairs untold,
How many autumns in our life are cold!
My corridor is loud with wind-blown leaves at night.
See my brows frown and hair turn white!

Of my poor wine few guests are proud;
The bright moon is oft veiled in cloud.
Who would enjoy with me the mid-autumn moon lonely?
Winecup in hand, northward I look only.

◀ 西江月　黄州中秋 | 洪健 绘
The Moon over the West River | Painter: Hong Jian

一葉舟輕 双槳鴻驚 水天清 影湛波平

行香子｜过七里濑

苏轼

一叶舟轻，双桨鸿惊。水天清、影湛波平。鱼翻藻鉴，鹭点烟汀。过沙溪急，霜溪冷，月溪明。

重重似画，曲曲如屏。算当年、虚老严陵。君臣一梦，今古空名。但远山长，云山乱，晓山青。

◀ **行香子 过七里濑**｜丁筱芳 绘
Song of Incense | Painter: Ding Xiaofang

Song of Incense

Passing the Seven-League Shallows

Su Shi

A leaflike boat goes light;
At dripping oars wild geese take fright.
Under a sky serene
Clear shadows float on calm waves green.
Among the mirrored water grass fish play
And egrets dot the riverbank mist-grey.
Thus I go past
The sandy brook flowing fast,
The frosted brook cold,
The moonlit brook bright to behold.

Hill upon hill is a picturesque scene;
Bend after bend looks like a screen.
I recall those far-away years:
The hermit wasted his life till he grew old;
The emperor shared the same dream with his peers.
Then as now, their fame was left out in the cold.
Only the distant hills outspread
Till they're unseen,
The cloud-crowned hills look disheveled
And dawnlit hills so green.

攜手江村梅雪飄
裙情何限處處消
魂故人不見舊曲重
聞向望湖樓孤山寺
湧金門
尋常行處題詩
千首繡羅衫與
拂紅塵別來相憶
知是何人有湖中
月江邊柳隴頭
雲蘇軾行香子
詞意

行香子

苏轼

携手江村，梅雪飘裙。情何限、处处消魂。故人不见，旧曲重闻。向望湖楼，孤山寺，涌金门。

寻常行处，题诗千首，绣罗衫、与拂红尘。别来相忆，知是何人。有湖中月，江边柳，陇头云。

Song of Incense

Su Shi

We visited the riverside village hand in hand,
Letting snowlike mume flowers on silk dress fall.
How can I stand
The soul-consuming fairy land!
Now separated from you for years long,
Hearing the same old song,
Can I forget the lakeside hall,
The temple on the Lonely Hill
And Golden Gate waves overfill?

Wherever we went on whatever day,
We have written a thousand lines.
The silken sleeves would sweep the dust away.
Since we parted, who
Would often think of you?
The moon which on the lake shines,
The lakeside willow trees,
The cloud and breeze.

暮云收尽溢清寒银汉无声转玉盘
此生此夜不长好明月明年何处看
苏轼阳关曲中秋

阳关曲｜中秋月

苏轼

暮云收尽溢清寒，银汉无声转玉盘。此生此夜不长好，明月明年何处看。

Song of the Sunny Pass

The Mid Autumn Moon

Su Shi

Evening clouds withdrawn, pure cold air floods the sky;
The River of Stars mute, a jade plate turns on high.
How oft can we enjoy a fine mid-autumn night?
Where shall we view next year a silver moon so bright?

◀ 阳关曲　中秋月｜庞飞 绘
Song of the Sunny Pass | Painter: Pang Fei

湖山信是东南美，一望弥千里。使君能得几回来？便是樽前醉倒更徘徊。细沙河塘里灯初上，水调谁家唱？夜阑风静欲归时，惟有一江明月碧琉璃。

甲午三月写东坡虞美人 海峰画并题

虞美人｜有美堂赠述古

苏轼

湖山信是东南美，一望弥千里。使君能得几回来，
便使樽前醉倒更徘徊。

沙河塘里灯初上，水调谁家唱。夜阑风静欲归时，
唯有一江明月碧琉璃。

The Beautiful Lady Yu

Written for Governor Chen at the Scenic Hall

Su Shi

How fair the lakes and hills of the Southern land are,
With plains extending wide and far!
How often, wine cup in hand, have you been here
That you can make us linger though drunk we appear!

By Sandy River Pool the new-lit lamps are bright.
Who is singing the water melody at night?
When I come back, the wind goes down, the bright moon paves
With emerald glass the river's waves.

◀ 虞美人　有美堂赠述古｜萧海春 绘
The Beautiful Lady Yu｜Painter: Xiao Haichun

鮑鷺

鹧鸪天

苏轼

林断山明竹隐墙。乱蝉衰草小池塘。翻空白鸟时时见，照水红蕖细细香。

村舍外，古城旁。杖藜徐步转斜阳。殷勤昨夜三更雨，又得浮生一日凉。

Partridges in the Sky

Su Shi

Through forest breaks appear hills and
Bamboo-screened wall;
Cicadas shrill o'er withered grass near a pool small.
White birds are seen now and then looping in the air;
Pink lotus blooms on lakeside exude fragrance spare.

Beyond the cots,
Near ancient town,
Cane in hand, I stroll round while the sun's slanting down.
Thanks to the welcome rain which fell when night was deep,
Now in my floating life one more flesh day I reap.

◀ 鹧鸪天 | 鲍莺 绘
Partridges in the Sky | Painter: Bao Ying

长相思

晏几道

长相思，长相思。若问相思甚了期，除非相见时。

长相思，长相思。欲把相思说似谁，浅情人不知。

Everlasting Longing

Yan Jidao

I yearn for long,
I yearn for long.
When may I end my yearning song?
Until you come along.

I yearn for long,
I yearn for long.
To whom may I sing my love song?
To none in love not strong.

◀ **长相思** | 丁筱芳 绘
Everlasting Longing | Painter: Ding Xiaofang

思远人

晏几道

红叶黄花秋意晚，千里念行客。飞云过尽，
归鸿无信，何处寄书得。

泪弹不尽临窗滴。就砚旋研墨。渐写到别来，
此情深处，红笺为无色。

Thinking of the Far-off One

Yan Jidao

Red leaves and yellow blooms fall, late autumn is done,
I think of my far-roving one.
Gazing on clouds blown away by the breeze
And messageless wild geese,
Where can I send him word under the sun?

My endless tears drip down by windowside
And blend with ink when they're undried.
I write down the farewell we bade;
My deep love impearled throws a shade
On rosy papers and they fade.

◀ 思远人 | 马小娟 绘
Thinking of the Far-off One | Painter: Ma Xiaojuan

浣溪沙

晏几道

二月和风到碧城，万条千缕绿相迎，舞烟眠雨过清明。

妆镜巧眉偷叶样，歌楼妍曲借枝名，晚秋霜霰莫无情。

Silk-Washing Stream

Yan Jidao

The gentle breeze of second moon has greened the town.
Thousands of your branches swing and sway up and down.
You dance in mist and sleep in rain on Mourning Day.

Ladies pencil their brows to imitate your leaf.
Songstresses sing your song to diminish their grief.
Late autumn frost, why delight in willows' decay?

◀ **浣溪沙** | 庞飞 绘
Silk-Washing Stream | Painter: Pang Fei

虞美人 | 宜州见梅作

黄庭坚

天涯也有江南信，梅破知春近。夜阑风细得香迟，
不道晓来开遍向南枝。

玉台弄粉花因妒，飘到眉心住。平生个里愿杯深，
去国十年老尽少年心。

The Beautiful Lady Yu

Huang Tingjian

Message comes from the south to the end of the sky,
When mumes burst open, spring is nigh.
At dead of night the wind is slight, your fragrance late.
Who knows at dawn your branches bloom at southern gate?

You're envied by powder of the Terrace of Jade;
You waft amid the brows and will not fade.
All my life long I love you with wine cup in hand;
My young heart oldens ten years away from homeland.

醉舞下山去明月逐人归

水调歌头

黄庭坚

瑶草一何碧，春入武陵溪。溪上桃花无数，枝上有黄鹂。我欲穿花寻路，直入白云深处，浩气展虹霓。只恐花深里，红露湿人衣。

坐玉石，倚玉枕，拂金徽。谪仙何处，无人伴我白螺杯。我为灵芝仙草，不为朱唇丹脸，长啸亦何为。醉舞下山去，明月逐人归。

◀ 水调歌头 | 丁筱芳 绘
Prelude to Water Melody | Painter: Ding Xiaofang

Prelude to Water Melody

Huang Tingjian

How could grass be so green? O Spring
Enters the fairy stream,
Where countless peach blooms beam,
And on the branch of the tree golden orioles sing.
I try to find a way through the flowers so gay,
Straight into clouds so white
To breathe a rainbow bright,
But I'm afraid in the depth of the flowers in my view,
My sleeves would be wet with rosy dew.

I sit on a stone and
Lean on a pillow of jade,
A tune on golden lute is played.
Where is the poet of the fairyland?
Who would drink up with me my spiral cup?
I come to seek for the immortal's trace,
Not for the rouged lips and powdered face.
Why should I long, long croon?
Drunk, I would dance downhill soon,
Followed by the bright moon.

忆故人 | 韩硕 绘 ▶
Old Friends Recalled: Han Shuo

忆故人

王诜

烛影摇红，向夜阑，乍酒醒、心情懒。尊前谁为唱阳关，离恨天涯远。

无奈云沉雨散。凭阑干、东风泪眼。海棠开后，燕子来时，黄昏庭院。

Old Friends Recalled

Wang Shen

The candle flickers red
At dead of night,
I wake from wine in bed,
My mind in idle plight.
Who sings before a cup of wine songs of goodbye?
My parting grief goes as far as the sky.

What can I do after you brought fresh shower
For my thirsting flower?
I lean on balustrade,
In eastern breeze my eyes shed tears.
When the crabapple flowers fade,
The swallow disappears,
The evening is hard in my courtyard.

烟水茫茫千里斜阳暮

点绛唇

秦观

醉漾轻舟，信流引到花深处。尘缘相误。无计花间住。

烟水茫茫，千里斜阳暮。山无数。乱红如雨。不记来时路。

Rouged Lips

Qin Guan

Drunk, at random I float
Along the stream my little boat.
By misfortune, among
The flowers I cannot stay long.

Misty waters outspread,
I find the slanting sun on turning my head,
And countless mountains high.
Red flowers fall in showers,
I don't remember the way I came by.

◀ **点绛唇**｜蔡天雄 绘
Rouged Lips | Painter: Cai Tianxiong

行到小溪深处
甲午夏 震文

好事近

秦观

春路雨添花，花动一山春色。行到小溪深处，
有黄鹂千百。

飞云当面化龙蛇，夭矫转空碧。醉卧古藤阴下，
了不知南北。

Song of Good Event

Qin Guan

The spring rain hastens roadside flowers to grow;
They undulate and fill mountains with spring.
Deep, deep along the stream I go,
And hear hundreds of orioles sing.

Flying cloud in my face turns to dragon or snake,
And swiftly melts in azure sky.
Lying drunk 'neath old vines, I can't make
Out if it's north or south by and by.

好事近 | 乐震文 绘
Song of Good Event | Painter: Le Zhenwen

臨江仙詞意
甲午

临江仙

秦观

千里潇湘挼蓝浦，兰桡昔日曾经。月高风定露华清。微波澄不动，冷浸一天星。

独倚危樯情悄悄，遥闻妃瑟泠泠。新声含尽古今情。曲终人不见，江上数峰青。

Riverside Daffodils

Qin Guan

I roam along the thousand-mile blue river-shore,
Where floated Poet Qu's orchid boat of yore.
The moon is high, the wind goes down, the dew is clear.
Ripples tranquil appear,
A skyful of stars shiver.

Silent, leaning against the high mast on the river,
I seem to hear the lute of the fairy queen.
Her music moves all hearts now as before.
When her song ends, she is not seen,
Leaving, on the stream but peaks green.

◀ 临江仙 | 朱敏 绘
Riverside Daffodils | Painter: Zhu Min

山抹微雲天連衰草畫角聲斷譙門暫停征棹聊共引離尊多少蓬
萊舊事空首煙靄紛紛斜陽外寒鴉萬點流水繞孤村銷魂當此際香囊暗
解罗帶輕分謾贏得青樓薄幸名存此去何時見也襟袖上空惹啼痕傷情
處高望斷燈已黃昏
秦觀滿庭芳詞意圖

满庭芳

秦观

山抹微云，天连衰草，画角声断谯门。暂停征棹，聊共引离尊。多少蓬莱旧事，空回首、烟霭纷纷。斜阳外，寒鸦万点，流水绕孤村。

消魂。当此际，香囊暗解，罗带轻分。谩赢得，青楼薄幸名存。此去何时见也，襟袖上、空惹啼痕。伤情处，高城望断，灯火已黄昏。

◀ **满庭芳**｜汪家芳 绘
Courtyard Full of Fragrance｜Painter: Wang Jiafang

Courtyard Full of Fragrance

Qin Guan

A belt of clouds girds mountains high
And withered grass spreads to the sky.
The painted horn at the watchtower blows.
Before my boat sails up,
Let's drink a farewell cup.
How many things do I recall in bygone days,
All lost in mist and haze!
Beyond the setting sun I see but dots of crows
And that around a lonely village water flows.

I'd call to mind the soul-consuming hour
When I took off your perfume purse unseen
And loosened your silk girdle in your bower.
All this has merely won me in the Mansion Green
The name of fickle lover.
Now I'm a rover,
O when can I see you again?
My tears are shed in vain;
In vain they wet my sleeves.
It grieves
My heart to find your bower out of sight;
It's lost at dusk in city light.

行香子 | 鲍莺 绘 ▶
Song of Incense | Painter: Bao Ying

鲍菁

行香子

秦观

树绕村庄，水满陂塘。倚东风、豪兴徜徉。小园几许，收尽春光。有桃花红，李花白，菜花黄。

远远苔墙，隐隐茅堂。飏青旗、流水桥旁。偶然乘兴，步过东冈。正莺儿啼，燕儿舞，蝶儿忙。

Song of Incense

Qin Guan

The village girt with trees,
The pools overbrim with water clear.
Leaning on eastern breeze,
My spirit soars up higher and freer.
The garden small
Has inhaled vernal splendor all:
Peach red, plums mellow
And rape flowers yellow.

Far off stand mossy walls,
Dim, dim the thatched halls,
The wineshop streamers fly;
Under the bridge water flows by.
By luck in spirits high
I pass where the eastern hills rise.
Orioles sing their song,
Swallows dance along,
Busy are butterflies.

鹊桥仙

秦观

纤云弄巧，飞星传恨，银汉迢迢暗渡。金风玉露一相逢，便胜却人间无数。

柔情似水，佳期如梦，忍顾鹊桥归路。两情若是久长时，又岂在朝朝暮暮。

Immortals at the Magpie Bridge

Qin Guan

Clouds float like works of art,
Stars shoot with grief at heart.
Across the Milky Way the Cowherd meets the Maid.
When Autumn's Golden Wind embraces Dew of Jade,
All the love scenes on earth, however many, fade.

Their tender love flows like a stream;
Their happy date seems but a dream.
How can they bear a separate homeward way?
If love between both sides can last for aye,
Why need they stay together night and day?

◀ 鹊桥仙 | 鲍莺 绘
Immortals at the Magpie Bridge | Painter: Bao Ying

烟水晚风恬落归帆

梦江南

贺铸

九曲池头三月三，柳毵毵。香尘扑马喷金衔，
涴春衫。

苦笋鲥鱼乡味美，梦江南。阊门烟水晚风恬，
落归帆。

Dreaming of the South

He Zhu

By winding stream with pools in third moon on third day,
The willow branches sway.
Fragrant dust is raised by spitting steeds with golden bit
And vernal dress is stained with spit.

I dream of the south.
How delicious are fish and bamboo shoots to the mouth!
The evening breeze calms misty waves before the town,
Returning sails lowered down.

◀ 梦江南 | 蔡天雄 绘
Dreaming of the South | Painter: Cai Tianxiong

踏荷行

踏莎行｜荷花

贺铸

杨柳回塘，鸳鸯别浦。绿萍涨断莲舟路。断无蜂蝶慕幽香，红衣脱尽芳心苦。

返照迎潮，行云带雨。依依似与骚人语。当年不肯嫁东风，无端却被秋风误。

踏莎行　荷花｜丁筱芳 绘
Treading on Grass | Painter: Ding Xiaofang

Treading on Grass

To Lotus

He Zhu

On winding pool with willows dim,
At narrow strait the lovebirds swim.
Green duckweeds float,
Barring the way of lotus-picking boat.
Nor butterflies nor bees
Love fragrance from the withered trees.
When her red petals fall apart,
The lotus bloom's bitter at heart.

The setting sun greets rising tide,
The floating clouds bring rain.
The swaying lotus seems to confide
Her sorrow to the poet in vain.
Then she would not be wed to vernal breeze,
What could she do now autumn drives away wild geese?

台城游 | 朱新昌 绘 ▶
The Terrace Wall | Painter: Zhu Xinchang

台城游

贺铸

南国本潇洒，六代浸豪奢。台城游冶，襞笺能赋属宫娃。云观登临清夏，璧月流连长夜，吟醉送年华。回首飞鸳瓦，却羡井中蛙。

访乌衣，成白社，不容车。旧时王谢，堂前双燕过谁家。楼外河横斗挂，淮上潮平霜下，墙影落寒沙。商女篷窗罅，犹唱后庭花。

The Terrace Wall

He Zhu

Gallant the Southern land far and wide,
Six Dynasties in opulence vied.
Wine, woman and song on Terrace Wall,
Eight beauties wrote verse in palace hall.
In summer clear they mounted the cloud-scraping height,
Under the jadelike moon they loitered in long night,
They drank and crooned the years away.
Leaving the lovebirds tiles pell-mell
They tried to hide like frogs in a well.

On street of mansions overgrown with grass
No cabs could pass.
The swallows in the mansions of bygone days,
In whose hall now do they stay?
Over the tower the Silver River bars the sky,
The Plough hangs high.
The tide runs up and down on frosty River Huai.
The shadow of townwalls on cold sand falls.
Through the window gap of the bower
I see the songstress sing the Backyard Flower.

吹盡繁紅占春長久不如垂柳
晁補之
水龍吟

水龙吟

晁补之

问春何苦匆匆，带风伴雨如驰骤。幽葩细萼，
小园低槛，壅培未就。吹尽繁红，占春长久。
不如垂柳。算春常不老，人愁春老，愁只是、
人间有。

春恨十常八九。忍轻辜、芳醪经口。那知自是，
桃花结子，不因春瘦。世上功名，老来风味，
春归时候。最多情犹有。尊前青眼，相逢依旧。

水龙吟｜何曦 绘
Water Dragon Chant | Painter: He Xi

Water Dragon Chant

Chao Buzhi

Why should spring go so soon, indeed,
With wind and rain like a galloping steed?
The flowers sweet in garden small
Are not deep planted in the soil at all.
Red blossoms will be blown down by the breeze;
They cannot last longer than willow trees.
Spring won't old grow.
How can it bring woe?
For weal and woe
Only in human world go.

Nine out of ten people regret spring's fleet.
Should we neglect a mouthful of wine sweet?
The peach tree won't grow thin for spring
But for the fruit which it will bring.
Do not sigh for glory on the decline
Till old are you
Or till spring says adieu.
Only a bosom friend
Before a cup of wine
Will last to the end.

迷神引 贬玉溪对江山作 | 蔡天雄 绘 ▶
Song of Enchantment | Painter: Cai Tianxiong

踏踏青山红日暮
浩浩大江东注余霞散绮

迷神引｜贬玉溪对江山作

晁补之

黯黯青山红日暮。浩浩大江东注。余霞散绮，向烟波路。使人愁，长安远，在何处。几点渔灯小，迷近坞。一片客帆低，傍前浦。

暗想平生，自悔儒冠误。觉阮途穷，归心阻。断魂素月，一千里、伤平楚。怪竹枝歌，声声怨，为谁苦。猿鸟一时啼，惊岛屿。烛暗不成眠，听津鼓。

Song of Enchantment

Written in Banishment

Chao Buzhi

Dim, dim the mountains blue, red, red the setting sun;
The boundless, endless river waves eastward run.
The rainbow clouds like brocade spread
Seem to flow on the misty waves going ahead
It grieves me
To leave the capital
I cannot see.
A few dots of fishing lanterns small
Flicker in the docks near the town,
By riverside sails lowered down.

Thinking of bygone days,
I regret to have lost my ways.
If I can't farther roam,
Why not go home?
Heart-broken to see the moon wane,
I'm grieved to view the far-flung plain
Stretched for a thousand Li.
The bamboo branch song grieves me.
For whom should it complain?
Monkeys and crows cry on the river,
Even the islets shiver.
In dimming candlelight I can't fall asleep
But hears the ferry drums announce that night is deep.

一一風荷舉
桂銘作

苏幕遮

周邦彦

燎沉香，消溽暑。鸟雀呼晴，侵晓窥檐语。
叶上初阳干宿雨，水面清圆，一一风荷举。

故乡遥，何日去。家住吴门，久作长安旅。
五月渔郎相忆否，小楫轻舟，梦入芙蓉浦。

◀ 苏幕遮 | 张桂铭 绘
Waterbag Dance | Painter: Zhang Guiming

Waterbag Dance

Zhou Bangyan

I burn an incense sweet
To temper steamy heat.
Birds chirp at dawn beneath the eaves,
Announcing a fine day. The rising sun
Has dried last night's raindrops on the lotus leaves,
Which, clear and round, dot water surface. One by one
The lotus blooms stand up with ease
And swing in morning breeze.

My homeland's far away;
When to return and stay?
My kinsfolk live in south by city wall.
Why should I linger long in the capital?
Will not my fishing friends remember me in May?
In a short-oared light boat, it seems,
I'm back 'mid lotus blooms in dreams.

念奴娇 | 朱敏 绘 ▶
Charm of a Maiden Singer | Painter: Zhu Min

念奴娇

念奴娇

叶梦得

云峰横起，障吴关三面，真成尤物。倒卷回潮，目尽处、秋水黏天无壁。绿鬓人归，如今虽在，空有千茎雪。追寻如梦，满余诗句犹杰。

闻道尊酒登临，孙郎终古恨，长歌时发。万里云屯，瓜步晚、落日旌旗明灭。鼓吹风高，画船遥想，一笑吞穷髪。当时曾照，更谁重问山月。

Charm of a Maiden Singer

Ye Mengde

Cloudy peaks bar the sky,
Screening three sides of Kingdom Wu,
A marvel on high.
The tide flows out as far as I stretch my eye,
The autumn water like a wall blends with the blue.
I left the town with black hair; now I come again
With a thousand stems of snow-white hair in vain.
The past gone like a dream,
My verse would pour out as a stream.

’T is said young General Sun oft came here with wine
And crooned verse fine.
To our regret early he died.
Clouds spread for miles and miles over the riverside;
The setting sun cast light and shade on Melon Isle.
With the drumbeats the wind runs high;
In my painted boat my thoughts fly.
When can we beat the foe with smiles?
The moon has shone on heroes of yore,
But who would care for heroes any more?

幸遇三杯酒好 況逢一朵花新 朱敦儒詞意何巧寫

西江月

朱敦儒

世事短如春梦，人情薄似秋云。不须计较苦劳心，万事原来有命。

幸遇三杯酒好，况逢一朵花新。片时欢笑且相亲，明日阴晴未定。

The Moon over the West River

Zhu Dunru

Life is as short as a spring dream;
Love is fleeting like autumn stream.
Don't on gain or loss speculate!
We can't avoid our fate.

I'm lucky to have three cups of good wine.
What's more, I can enjoy fresh flower.
Make merry in laughter for an hour.
Who knows if tomorrow it will be fine.

◀ **西江月** | 何曦 绘
The Moon over the West River | Painter: He Xi

笛聲三弄
梅心驚破
多少遊春意
李清照詞
意圖
甲午小秋於
海上半
裡園佳製

孤雁儿

李清照

藤床纸帐朝眠起，说不尽、无佳思。沉香断续玉炉寒，伴我情怀如水。笛声三弄，梅心惊破，多少游春意。

小风疏雨萧萧地，又催下、千行泪。吹箫人去玉楼空，肠断与谁同倚。一枝折得，人间天上，没个人堪寄。

◀ **孤雁儿**｜洪健 绘
A Lonely Swan | Painter: Hong Jian

A Lonely Swan

Li Qingzhao

Woke up at dawn on cane-seat couch with silken screen,
How can I tell my endless sorrow keen?
With incense burnt, the censer cold
Keeps company with my stagnant heart as of old.
The flute thrice played
Breaks the mume's vernal heart which vernal thoughts invade.

A grizzling wind and drizzling rain
Call forth streams of tears again.
The flutist gone, deserted is the bower of jade
Who'd lean with me, broken-hearted, on the balustrade?
A twig of mume blossoms broken off, to whom can I
Send it, on earth or on high?

声声慢 | 马小娟 绘 ▶
Slow, Slow Tune | Painter: Ma Xiaojuan

声声慢

李清照

寻寻觅觅，冷冷清清，凄凄惨惨戚戚。乍暖还寒时候，最难将息。三杯两盏淡酒，怎敌他、晚来风急。雁过也，正伤心，却是旧时相识。

满地黄花堆积。憔悴损，如今有谁堪摘。守着窗儿，独自怎生得黑。梧桐更兼细雨，到黄昏、点点滴滴。这次第，怎一个愁字了得。

Slow, Slow Tune

Li Qingzhao

I look for what I miss;
I know not what it is.
I feel so sad, so drear,
So lonely, without cheer.
How hard is it
To keep me fit
In this lingering cold!
Hardly warmed up
By cup on cup
Of wine so dry,
O how could I
Endure at dusk the drift
Of wind so swift?
It breaks my heart, alas!
To see the wild geese pass,
For they are my acquaintances of old.

The ground is covered with yellow flowers,
Faded and fallen in showers.
Who will pick them up now?
Sitting alone at the window, how
Could I but quicken
The pace of darkness that won't thicken?
On plane's broad leaves a fine rain drizzles
As twilight grizzles.
O what can I do with a grief
Beyond belief?

鮑鷺

一剪梅

李清照

红藕香残玉簟秋。轻解罗裳，独上兰舟。
云中谁寄锦书来，雁字回时，月满西楼。

花自飘零水自流。一种相思，两处闲愁。
此情无计可消除，才下眉头，却上心头。

A Twig of Mume Blossoms

Li Qingzhao

Fragrant lotus blooms fade, autumn chills mat of jade.
My silk robe doffed, I float
Alone in orchid boat.
Who in the cloud would bring me letters in brocade?
When swans come back in flight,
My bower is steeped in moonlight.

As fallen flowers drift and water runs its way,
One longing leaves no traces
O how can such lovesickness be driven away?
From eyebrows kept apart,
Again it gnaws my heart.

◀ 一剪梅 | 鲍莺 绘
A Twig of Mume Blossoms | Painter: Bao Ying

鮑鷺

醉花阴

李清照

薄雾浓云愁永昼，瑞脑消金兽。佳节又重阳，
玉枕纱厨，半夜凉初透。

东篱把酒黄昏后，有暗香盈袖。莫道不销魂，
帘卷西风，人比黄花瘦。

◀ **醉花阴** | 鲍莺 绘
Tipsy in the Flowers' Shade | Painter: Bao Ying

Tipsy in the Flowers' Shade

Li Qingzhao

Veiled in thin mist and thick cloud, how sad the long day!
Incense from golden censer melts away.
The Double Ninth comes again;
Alone I still remain
In silken bed curtain, on pillow smooth like jade.
Feeling the midnight chill invade.

At dusk I drink before chrysanthemums in bloom,
My sleeves filled with fragrance and gloom.
Say not my soul
Is not consumed. Should the west wind uproll
The curtain of my bower,
You'll see a face thinner than yellow flower.

虞美人 | 洪健 绘 ▶
The Beautiful Lady Yu | Painter: Hong Jian

一路繁花相送过青墩
甲午夏日

虞美人

陈与义

余甲寅岁自春官出守湖州，秋杪，道中荷花无复存者。乙卯岁，自琐闼以病得请奉祠，卜居青墩镇。立秋后三日行，舟之前后如朝霞相映，望之不断也。以长短句记之。

扁舟三日秋塘路，平度荷花去。病夫因病得来游，更值满川微雨洗新秋。

去年长恨拏舟晚，空见残荷满。今年何以报君恩，一路繁花相送过青墩。

The Beautiful Lady Yu

Chen Yuyi

Three days after the Autumn Day
My boat goes along the lotus poolside way.
Ill, I come for an autumn view;
The drizzling rain has washed clear autumn new.

Last year's regret of coming late would still remain;
I saw but withered blooms in vain.
How should I show my gratitude this year,
When all the way flowers in bloom appear?

满江红

岳飞

怒发冲冠，凭阑处、潇潇雨歇。抬望眼、仰天长啸，壮怀激烈。三十功名尘与土，八千里路云和月。莫等闲、白了少年头，空悲切。

靖康耻，犹未雪。臣子恨，何时灭。驾长车踏破、贺兰山缺。壮志饥餐胡虏肉，笑谈渴饮匈奴血。待从头、收拾旧山河，朝天阙。

◀ 满江红 | 丁筱芳 绘
The River All Red | Painter: Ding Xiaofang

The River All Red

Yue Fei

Wrath sets on end my hair;
I lean on railings where
I see the drizzling rain has ceased.
Raising my eyes
Towards the skies,
I heave long sighs,
My wrath not yet appeased.
To dust is gone the fame achieved in thirty years;
Like cloud-veiled moon the thousand-mile Plain disappears.
Should youthful heads in vain turn grey,
We would regret for aye.

Lost our capitals,
What a burning shame!
How can we generals
Quench our vengeful flame!
Driving our chariots of war, we'd go
To break through our relentless foe.
Valiantly we'd cut off each head;
Laughing, we'd drink the blood they shed.
When we've reconquered our lost land,
In triumph would return our army grand.

小重山 | 朱敏 绘 ▶
Manifold Little Hills | Painter: Zhu Min

小重山

岳飞

昨夜寒蛩不住鸣。惊回千里梦，已三更。起来独自绕阶行。人悄悄，帘外月胧明。

白首为功名。旧山松竹老，阻归程。欲将心事付瑶琴。知音少，弦断有谁听。

Manifold Little Hills

Yue Fei

The autumn crickets chirped incessantly last night,
Breaking my dream homebound;
'T was already midnight.
I got up and alone in the yard walked around;
On window screen the moon shone bright;
There was no human sound.

My hair turns grey
For the glorious day.
In native hills bamboos and pines grow old.
O when can I see my household?
I would confide to my lute what I have in view,
But connoisseurs are few.
Who would be listening,
Though I break my lute string?

驛外斷橋邊寂寞開無主已是黃昏
獨自愁更著風和雨無意苦爭春一任
群芳妒零落成泥輾作塵祇有香
如故 畫陸游卜算子詠梅於雲巖之
畔臥雲居歲在甲午年六月六日
金陵高雲併記

卜算子 | 咏梅

陆游

驿外断桥边，寂寞开无主。已是黄昏独自愁，
更著风和雨。

无意苦争春，一任群芳妒。零落成泥碾作尘，
只有香如故。

Song of Divination

Ode to the Mume Blossom

Lu You

Beside the broken bridge and outside the post hall
A flower is blooming forlorn.
Saddened by her solitude at nightfall,
By wind and rain she's further torn.

Let other flowers their envy pour!
To spring she lays no claim.
Fallen in mud and ground to dust, she seems no more,
But her fragrance is still the same.

◀ 卜算子　咏梅 | 高云 绘
Song of Divination | Painter: Gao Yun

蝶恋花

陆游

桐叶晨飘蛩夜语。旅思秋光，黯黯长安路。
忽记横戈盘马处。散关清渭应如故。

江海轻舟今已具。一卷兵书，叹息无人付。
早信此生终不遇。当年悔草长杨赋。

Butterflies in Love with Flowers

Lu You

The plane's leaves fall at dawn and crickets chirp at night
In dreary autumn light.
Leaving for capital, I make my gloomy way,
Remembering the day
When I rode on my horse and wielded my spear.
The Western Pass should stand still and the stream as clear.

I would float on the sea as I wished before.
To whom can I confide my book on the art of war?
If I had known I'd meet in life no connoisseur,
Why should I have advised in vain the emperor?

◀ **蝶恋花**｜朱新昌 绘
Butterflies in Love with Flowers | Painter: Zhu Xinchang

三年流落巴山道破尽青衫尘满帽
陆游木兰花立春日作词一首

木兰花 | 立春日作

陆游

三年流落巴山道。破尽青衫尘满帽。身如西瀼
渡头云，愁抵瞿塘关上草。

春盘春酒年年好。试戴银旛判醉倒。今朝一岁
大家添，不是人间偏我老。

Magnolia Flowers

Spring Day

Lu You

A roamer from the east to the west for three years,
Worn out in my blue gown, dusty my hat appears.
Like floating cloud over the ferry of west stream,
Or grass overgrown in Three Gorges, my grief would seem.

From year to year spring plate is as good as spring wine;
We vie to be drunk adorned with ribbons fine.
All of us have grown older by one year today;
I'm not the only one to olden in my way.

◀ 木兰花　立春日作 | 庞飞 绘
Magnolia Flowers | Painter: Pang Fei

昭君怨｜咏荷上雨

杨万里

午梦扁舟花底，香满西湖烟水。急雨打篷声，梦初惊。

却是池荷跳雨，散了真珠还聚。聚作水银窝，泛清波。

Lament of a Fair Lady

Raindrops on Lotus Leaves

Yang Wanli

I nap at noon in a leaflike boat beneath lotus flowers;
Their fragrance spreads over mist-veiled West Lake.
I hear my boat's roof beaten by sudden showers,
And startled, I awake.

I find on lotus leaves leap drops of rain;
Like pearls they scatter and get together again.
They melt then into liquid silver
Flowing down the rippling river.

◀ 昭君怨 咏荷上雨｜何曦 绘
Lament of a Fair Lady | Painter:He Xi

念奴娇｜过洞庭

张孝祥

洞庭青草，近中秋、更无一点风色。玉鉴琼田
三万顷，着我扁舟一叶。素月分辉，明河共影，
表里俱澄澈。悠然心会，妙处难与君说。

应念岭表经年，孤光自照，肝胆皆冰雪。短发萧
疏襟袖冷，稳泛沧溟空阔。尽挹西江，细斟北斗，
万象为宾客。扣舷独啸，不知今夕何夕。

Charm of a Maiden Singer

Zhang Xiaoxiang

Lake Dongting, Lake Green Grass,
Near the Mid-autumn night,
Unruffled for no winds pass,
Like thirty thousand acres of jade bright
Dotted with the leaflike boat of mine.
The skies with pure moonbeams o'erflow;
The water surface paved with moonshine:
Brightness above, brightness below.
My heart with the moon becomes one,
Felicity to share with none.

Thinking of the southwest, where I passed a year,
To lonely pure moonlight skin,
I feel my heart and soul snow-and-ice-clear.
Although my hair is short and sparse, my gown too thin,
In the immense expanse I keep floating up.
Drinking wine from the River West
And using Dipper as wine cup,
I invite Nature to be my guest.
Beating time aboard and crooning alone.
I sink deep into time and place unknown.

水调歌头　金山观月 | 朱敏 绘 ▶
Prelude to Water Melody | Painter: Zhu Min

金山观月词意

水调歌头｜金山观月

张孝祥

江山自雄丽，风露与高寒。寄声月姊，借我玉鉴此中看。幽壑鱼龙悲啸，倒影星辰摇动，海气夜漫漫。涌起白银阙，危驻紫金山。

表独立，飞霞珮，切云冠。漱冰濯雪，眇视万里一毫端。回首三山何处，闻道群仙笑我，要我欲俱还。挥手从此去，翳凤更骖鸾。

Prelude to Water Melody

The Moon Viewed on Golden Hill

Zhang Xiaoxiang

The lofty mountain stands in view,
When wind is high and cold is dew.
I'd ask the Goddess of the Moon
To lend me her jade mirror soon
To see in deep water fish and dragon sigh
And stars shiver as if fallen from on high.
The boundless sea mingles her breath with boundless night.
On the waves surges the palace silver-white;
The Golden Hill Temple frowns on the height.

Alone it towers high,
Girt with a rainbow bright,
Its crown would scrape the sky.
With ice and snow purified,
It overlooks the boundless land far and wide.
Looking back; where are the fairy hills two or three?
The immortals may laugh at me;
They ask me to go with them to the sea.
Waving my hand,
I'll leave the land
With a phoenix as my canopy.

八声甘州

辛弃疾

夜读《李广传》，不能寐。因念晁楚老、杨民瞻约同居山间，戏用李广事，赋以寄之。

故将军饮罢夜归来，长亭解雕鞍。恨灞陵醉尉，匆匆未识，桃李无言。射虎山横一骑，裂石响惊弦。落魄封侯事，岁晚田间。

谁向桑麻杜曲，要短衣匹马，移住南山。看风流慷慨，谈笑过残年。汉开边、功名万里，甚当时、健者也曾闲。纱窗外、斜风细雨，一阵轻寒。

◀ 八声甘州 | 朱新昌 绘
Eight Beats of Ganzhou Song | Painter: Zhu Xinchang

Eight Beats of Ganzhou Song

On Reading General Li Guang's Biography

Xin Qiji

The Flying General was famed for his force.
When drunk, he came back at night,
At Long Pavilion unsaddled his horse.
But the officer drunk knew not the hero bright,
So the general stood without speech
Like plum or peach.
His galloping steed
Crossed the mountain in speed,
Taking a rock for a tiger, he twanged his string tight
And pierced the stone.
Not ennobled late in years, unknown,
He lived in countryside, alone.

Who would live in the fields with wine,
In short coat or on a horse fine,
And move to the foot of the southern hill?
Valiant and fervent still,
I'd pass in laughter the rest of my years.
On the thousand-mile-long frontiers,
How many generals won a name!
But the strongest was not ennobled with his fame.
Out of my window screen the slanting breeze
And drizzling rain would freeze.

破阵子｜施大畏 绘 ▶
Dance of the Cavalry | Painter: Shi Dawei

破阵子

辛弃疾

醉里挑灯看剑，梦回吹角连营。八百里分麾下炙，
五十弦翻塞外声。沙场秋点兵。

马作的卢飞快，弓如霹雳弦惊。了却君王天下事，
赢得生前身后名。可怜白发生。

Dance of the Cavalry

Xin Qiji

Though drunk, we lit the lamp to see the glaive;
Sober, we heard the horns from tent to tent.
Under the flags, beef grilled
Was eaten by our warriors brave
And martial airs were played by fifty instruments:
'T was an autumn manoeuvre in the field.

On gallant steed,
Running fun speed,
We'd shoot with twanging bows
Recovering the lost land for the sovereign,
'T is everlasting fame that we would win.
But alas! White hair grows!

清平乐 | 村居

辛弃疾

茅檐低小，溪上青青草。醉里吴音相媚好，白发谁家翁媪。

大儿锄豆溪东，中儿正织鸡笼。最喜小儿无赖，溪头卧剥莲蓬。

Pure Serene Music

Xin Qiji

The thatched roof slants low,
Beside the brook green grasses grow.
Who talks with drunken Southern voice to please?
White-haired man and wife at their ease.

East of the brook their eldest son is hoeing weeds;
Their second son now makes a cage for hens he feeds.
How pleasant to see their spoiled youngest son who heeds
Nothing but lies by brookside and pods lotus seeds!

◀ 清平乐　村居 | 朱新昌 绘
Pure Serene Music | Painter: Zhu Xinchang

清平乐｜独宿博山王氏庵

辛弃疾

绕床饥鼠，蝙蝠翻灯舞。屋上松风吹急雨，破纸窗间自语。

平生塞北江南，归来华发苍颜。布被秋宵梦觉，眼前万里江山。

Pure Serene Music

Xin Qiji

Around the bed run hungry rats;
In lamplight to and fro fly bats.
On pine-shaded roof the wind and shower rattle;
The window paper scraps are heard to prattle.

I roam from north to south, from place to place,
And come back with grey hair and wrinkled face.
I woke up in thin quilt on autumn night;
The boundless land I dreamed of still remains in sight.

◀ 清平乐　独宿博山王氏庵｜江宏 绘
Pure Serene Music | Painter: Jiang Hong

清平乐｜检校山园，书所见

辛弃疾

连云松竹，万事从今足。拄杖东家分社肉，白酒床头初熟。

西风梨枣山园，儿童偷把长竿。莫遣旁人惊去，老夫静处闲看。

Pure Serene Music

Hillside Garden

Xin Qiji

Bamboos and pines extend to the clouds far and wide:
From now on, with all I am satisfied
Cane in hand, I go east to take my share of meat:
At the head of my bed the first brew of wine sweet.

The west wind ripens pears and dates in hillside land:
Children come stealthily, long pole in hand.
Do not scare them out of their pleasure!
I will sit quietly at leisure.

◀ 清平乐　检校山园，书所见｜朱新昌 绘
Pure Serene Music | Painter: Zhu Xinchang

水龙吟｜登建康赏心亭

辛弃疾

楚天千里清秋，水随天去秋无际。遥岑远目，
献愁供恨，玉簪螺髻。落日楼头，断鸿声里，
江南游子。把吴钩看了，阑干拍遍，无人会、
登临意。

休说鲈鱼堪脍，尽西风、季鹰归未。求田问舍，
怕应羞见，刘郎才气。可惜流年，忧愁风雨，
树犹如此。倩何人，唤取红巾翠袖，揾英雄泪。

◀ 水龙吟　登建康赏心亭｜蔡天雄 绘
Water Dragon Chant | Painter: Cai Tianxiong

Water Dragon Chant

Xin Qiji

The Southern sky for miles and miles in autumn dye
And boundless autumn water spread to meet the sky,
I gaze on far-off northern hills
Like spiral shells or hair decor of jade,
Which grief or hatred overfills.
Leaning at sunset on balustrade
And hearing a lonely swan's song,
A wanderer on southern land,
I look at my precious sword long
And pound all the railings with my hand,
But nobody knows why
I climb the tower high.

Don't say for food
The perch is good!
When west winds blow,
Why don't I homeward go?
I'd be ashamed to see the patriot,
Should I retire to seek for land and cot.
I sigh for passing years I can't retain;
In driving wind and blinding rain
Even an old tree grieves.
To whom then may I say
To wipe my tears away
With her pink handkerchief or her green sleeves?

永遇乐　京口北固亭怀古 | 朱敏 绘 ▶
Joy of Eternal Union | Painter: Zhu Min

永遇乐｜京口北固亭怀古

辛弃疾

千古江山，英雄无觅，孙仲谋处。舞榭歌台，
风流总被，雨打风吹去。斜阳草树，寻常巷陌，
人道寄奴曾住。想当年，金戈铁马，气吞万里
如虎。

元嘉草草，封狼居胥，赢得仓皇北顾。四十三年，
望中犹记，烽火扬州路。可堪回首，佛狸祠下，
一片神鸦社鼓。凭谁问，廉颇老矣，尚能饭否。

Joy of Eternal Union

Xin Qiji

The land is boundless as of yore,
But nowhere can be found
A hero like the king defending southern shore.
The singing hall, the dancing ground,
All gallant deeds now sent away
By driving wind and blinding rain!
The slanting sun sheds its departing ray
O'er tree-shaded and grassy lane
Where lived the Cowherd King retaking the lost land.
In bygone years,
Leading armed cavaliers,
With golden spear in hand
Tigerlike, he had slain
The foe on the thousand-mile Central Plain.

His son launched in haste a northern campaign;
Defeated at Mount Wolf, he shed his tears in vain.
I still remember three and forty years ago
The thriving town destroyed in flames by the foe.
How can I bear
To see the chief aggressor's shrine
Worshipped 'mid crows and drumbeats as divine?
Who would still care
If an old general
Is strong enough to take back the lost capital?

試寫辛棄疾夜行黃沙道中詞意 何

西江月 | 夜行黄沙道中

辛弃疾

明月别枝惊鹊，清风半夜鸣蝉。稻花香里说丰年，
听取蛙声一片。

七八个星天外，两三点雨山前。旧时茅店社林边，
路转溪桥忽见。

The Moon over the West River

Xin Qiji

Startled by magpies leaving the branch in moonlight,
I hear cicadas shrill in the breeze at midnight.
The ricefields' sweet smell promises a bumper year;
Listen, how frogs' croaks please the ear!

Beyond the clouds seven or eight stars twinkle;
Before the hills two or three raindrops sprinkle.
There is an inn beside the village temple. Look!
The winding path leads to the hut beside the brook.

◀ 西江月　夜行黄沙道中 | 何曦 绘
The Moon over the West River | Painter: He Xi

甲午
辛弃疾
鹧鸪天
词意图

鹧鸪天｜游鹅湖，醉书酒家壁

辛弃疾

春入平原荠菜花。新耕雨后落群鸦。多情白发春无奈，晚日青帘酒易赊。

闲意态，细生涯。牛栏西畔有桑麻。青裙缟袂谁家女，去趁蚕生看外家。

Partridges in the Sky

Written on the Wall of a Wine Shop

Xin Qiji

Spring comes to the plain with shepherd's purse in flower,
A flock of crows fly down on new-filled fields after shower.
What could an old man with young heart do on days fine?
At dusk he drinks on credit in the shop of wine.

People with ease
Do what they please.
West of the cattle pen there're hemps and mulberries.
Why should the newly-wed in black skirt and white coat run
To see her parents before cocoons are spun?

◀ 鹧鸪天　游鹅湖，醉书酒家壁｜韩硕 绘
Partridges in the Sky | Painter: Han Shuo

鹧鸪天

辛弃疾

陌上柔桑破嫩芽。东邻蚕种已生些。平冈细草
鸣黄犊，斜日寒林点暮鸦。

山远近，路横斜。青旗沽酒有人家。城中桃李
愁风雨，春在溪头荠菜花。

Partridges in the Sky

Xin Qiji

The tender twigs begin to spout along the lane;
The silkworm's eggs of my east neighbor have come out.
The yellow calves grazing fine grass bawl on the plain;
At sunset in the cold forest crows fly about.

The mountains extend far and near;
Lanes crisscross there and here.
Blue streamers fly where wine shops appear.
Peach and plum blossoms in the town fear wind and showers,
But spring dwells by the creekside where blossom wildflowers.

◀ 鹧鸪天 | 江宏 绘
Partridges in the Sky | Painter: Jiang Hong

追往事叹今吾
春风不染白髭须

鹧鸪天

辛弃疾

有客慨然谈功名，因追念少年时事，戏作。

壮岁旌旗拥万夫。锦襜突骑渡江初。燕兵夜娖
银胡觮，汉箭朝飞金仆姑。

追往事，叹今吾。春风不染白髭须。却将万字
平戎策，换得东家种树书。

Partridges in the Sky

Xin Qiji

While young, beneath my flag I had ten thousand knights;
With these outfitted cavaliers I crossed the river.
The foe prepared their silver shafts during the nights;
During the days we shot arrows from golden quiver.

I can’t call those days back
But sigh over my plight;
The vernal wind can’t change my hair from white to black.
Since thwarted in my plan to recover the lost land,
I’d learn from neighbors how to plant fruit trees by hand.

◀ 鹧鸪天 | 丁筱芳 绘
Partridges in the Sky | Painter: Ding Xiaofang

把酒對斜日無語問西風胭脂何事
都做顏色染芙蓉 楊炎正詞

水调歌头

杨炎正

把酒对斜日，无语问西风。胭脂何事，都做颜色染芙蓉。放眼暮江千顷，中有离愁万斛，无处落征鸿。天在阑干角，人倚醉醒中。

千万里，江南北，浙西东。吾生如寄，尚想三径菊花丛。谁是中州豪杰，借我五湖舟楫，去作钓鱼翁。故国且回首，此意莫匆匆。

◀ **水调歌头** | 何曦 绘
Prelude to Water Melody | Painter: He Xi

Prelude to Water Melody

Yang Yanzheng

Wine cup in hand, I face the slanting sun;
Silent, I ask what the western wind has done.
Why should the rouge redden lotus in dye?
I stretch my eye
To see the evening river far and wide,
Brimming with parting grief
Beyond belief,
Where no message-bearing wild geese can alight.
Beyond the balustrade extends the sky.
I lean on it, halfdrunk and halfawake.

For miles and more
Over the north and south
Of the river mouth,
And east and west of the river shore,
I roam like a parasite.
Thinking of the chrysanthemums along the pathways,
Who is so generous in those days
To lend me a boat to float on the lake
Or fish by riverside?
Turning my head to gaze on the lost land,
How could I, doing nothing, here stand!

蘆葉滿汀洲
寒沙帶淺流
二十年重過南
樓柳下繫
船猶未穩能
幾日又中秋
劉改之唐多令
詞意
甲午春日

唐多令

刘过

安远楼小集，侑觞歌板之姬，黄其姓者，乞词于龙洲道人，为赋此《唐多令》。同柳阜之、刘去非、石民瞻、周嘉仲、陈孟参、孟容，时八月五日也。

芦叶满汀洲，寒沙带浅流。二十年重过南楼。
柳下系船犹未稳，能几日、又中秋。

黄鹤断矶头，故人今在否。旧江山浑是新愁。
欲买桂花同载酒，终不似、少年游。

Song of More Sugar

Liu Guo

Reeds overspread the small island;
A shallow stream girds the cold sand.
After twenty years
I pass by the Southern Tower again.
How many days have passed since I tied my boat
Beneath the willow tree! But Mid-Autumn Day nears.

On broken rocks of Yellow Crane,
Do my old friends still remain?
The old land is drowned in sorrow new.
Even if I can buy laurel wine for you
And get afloat,
Could our youth renew?

醉太平閨情詞意
甲午夏月於滬上西陽半隱園
健

醉太平｜闺情

刘过

情高意真，眉长鬓青。小楼明月调筝，写春风数声。

思君忆君，魂牵梦萦。翠销香减云屏，更那堪酒醒。

Drunk in Time of Peace

Liu Guo

With heart and mind aspiring high,
With eyebrows long and forehead dark,
In moonlit bower to play on zither I try.
O vernal wind, O hark!

I think of you, I long for you, unseen
Even in my dream, O beloved of mine!
When incense warms the mica screen,
What can I do when I'm awake from wine?

◀ 醉太平 闺情｜洪健 绘
Drunk in Time of Peace | Painter: Hong Jian

沁园春｜忆黄山

汪莘

三十六峰，三十六溪，长锁清秋。对孤峰绝顶，云烟竞秀；悬崖峭壁，瀑布争流。洞里桃花，仙家芝草，雪后春正取次游。亲曾见，是龙潭白昼，海涌潮头。

当年黄帝浮丘。有玉枕玉床还在不。向天都月夜，遥闻凤管；翠微霜晓，仰盼龙楼。砂穴长红，丹炉已冷，安得灵方闻早修。谁知此，问源头白鹿，水畔青牛。

Spring in a Pleasure Garden

Yellow Mountains Recalled

Wang Xin

Thirty-six peaks
And thirty-six streams
Have long locked clear autumn in dreams.
In face of lonely peaks and lofty crest,
Clouds and mist vie to look their best.
Over cliffs steep and high
Cascades in roaring vie.
In the cave grow peach flowers,
And life-long herbs in divine bowers.
After spring snow one by one they will come in sight.
I have seen with my eyes
The Dragon's Pool in broad daylight,
The sea in angry billows rise.

Of the Yellow Emperor's reign,
Do the jade bed and pillow still remain?
From the Celestial Town in moonlight,
I've heard the phoenix flute play music bright.
On green mountains in frosty morning hours,
I've looked up to Dragon's towers.
Still red is the elixir old,
But the Magical Stove is cold.
How could a mortal turn divine?
If you do want to know,
Ask the white deer at the source fine
Or the waterside buffalo.

东风第一枝　咏春雪 | 乐震文 绘
The First Branch in the Eastern Breeze | Painter: Le Zhenwen

东风第一枝｜咏春雪

史达祖

巧沁兰心，偷粘草甲，东风欲障新暖。谩凝碧瓦难留，信知暮寒轻浅。行天入镜，做弄出、轻松纤软。料故园、不卷重帘，误了乍来双燕。

青未了、柳回白眼。红欲断、杏开素面。旧游忆着山阴，后盟遂妨上苑。寒炉重熨，便放慢、春衫针线。怕凤靴、挑菜归来，万一灞桥相见。

The First Branch in the Eastern Breeze

To Spring Snow

Shi Dazu

Penetrating with art
Into the orchid's heart,
And clinging like a lass
To the leaves of grass,
The eastern breeze brings new warmth you try to delay.
Congealed on green tiles, you cannot long stay;
Coming late, we know you are thin and light.
Flying up or down to the mirror of the sky,
You seem to be soft and sly.
Seeing the undrawn screen in my hometown,
The swallows coming back would take it for place unknown.

The grass still green,
Willows turn white;
Apricot's rosy face
Is veiled with grace.
You beautify the friends' journey at night,
And delay poets' visit to garden scene.
The stove rekindled for you,
We may put off the sewing of spring garment new.
I fear I cannot meet
The beauty coming with vegetables sweet,
Then how could I seek my metrical feet?

烟梢月树
宋人史达祖
留春令咏
梅花词意
甲午

留春令｜咏梅花

史达祖

故人溪上，挂愁无奈，烟梢月树。一涓春水点黄昏，
便没顿、相思处。

曾把芳心深相许。故梦劳诗苦。闻说东风亦多情，
被竹外、香留住。

Retaining Spring

To Mume Flowers

Shi Dazu

Strolling along your streams,
What can I do but hang my grief and dream
On moonlit mist-veiled tree?
The vernal water threads through the twilight.
Of longing for you can I be free?

You have confided your love to me,
So I've lost labor in dreaming of verse bright.
It is said spring's as sentimental as you,
Retained by fragrance beyond the bamboo.

◄ 留春令　咏梅花｜庞飞 绘
Retaining Spring | Painter: Pang Fei

戴復古詞意赤壁懷古 華敏

满江红｜赤壁怀古

戴复古

赤壁矶头，一番过、一番怀古。想当时、周郎年少，
气吞区宇。万骑临江貔虎噪，千艘列炬鱼龙怒。
卷长波、一鼓困曹瞒，今如许。

江上渡，江边路。形胜地，兴亡处。览遗踪，
胜读史书言语。几度东风吹世换，千年往事随
潮去。问道傍、杨柳为谁春，摇金缕。

◀ 满江红　赤壁怀古｜朱敏 绘
The River All Red | Painter: Zhu Min

The River All Red

The Red Cliff

Dai Fugu

Passing the head of the Cliff Red,
Can I forget the bygone days,
When the young general spread his heroic rays?
Thousands of steeds roared like tigers by riverside;
Hundreds of ships in wrath with fish and dragon vied.
Rolling long wave on wave,
They beat the foe so brave.
What happens nowadays?

The ferry on the tide
And roads by riverside
Have witnessed all
Dynasties' rise and fall.
Seeing the relics of war,
We understand history all the more.
How many times has changed the world which raves!
A thousand years have passed away with the waves.
I ask the roadside willow trees:
"For whom are you swaying in vernal breeze?"

西河　和王潜斋韵｜朱敏 绘 ▶
The West River | Painter: Zhu Min

西河｜和王潜斋韵

曹豳

今日事，何人弄得如此。漫漫白骨蔽川原，恨何日已。关河万里寂无烟，月明空照芦苇。

谩哀痛，无及矣。无情莫问江水。西风落日惨新亭，几人堕泪。战和何者是良筹，扶危但看天意。

只今寂寞薮泽里，岂无人、高卧闾里。试问安危谁寄。定相将有诏催公起。须信前书言犹未。

The West River

In Reply to Wang Ye

Cao Bin

Today's affairs, my friend,
How can they come to such a state?
So many bleached bones are buried in the plain.
When can our grief come to an end?
For miles and miles no smoke rises from towns desolate.
The moon shines on the reeds in vain.

Our grief so deep cannot be drowned anew
In running water of the heartless stream.
The western breeze at sunset saddens the pavilion new.
Flow many would shed tears even in dream?
Should we seek peace or war? We could confide the state
only to the fate.

Could there be no heroes in the land far and wide?
They lie in bed, lonely in countryside.
On whom can we rely any more?
I wish you would rise as general
To lead the army to defend the capital.
Don't you believe what I have said before?

雲扉浸鏡空
山寒猿啼
斷松殘明
芝英安在求
嗇已老猿莠
巖畔花飛洞
中風蕭颯
瑟瑟常歇
吹帳卷菩提
香石門信
斷莖人間淡
歌事
節錄宋人
葛長庚家
菊花詞

甲午之歲五月於京中國畫院 寫

水龙吟｜采药径

葛长庚

云屏漫锁空山，寒猿啼断松枝翠。芝英安在，术苗已老，徒劳屐齿。应记洞中，凤箫锦瑟，镇常歌吹。怅苍苔路杳，石门信断，无人问、溪头事。

回首暝烟无际，但纷纷、落花如泪。多情易老，青鸾何处，书成难寄。欲问双娥，翠蝉金凤，向谁娇媚。想分香旧恨，刘郎去后，一溪流水。

Water Dragon Chant

Where Is the Wonderful Grass

Ge Changgeng

Clouds veil the empty mountains like a screen;
Cold monkeys cry on pine branches green.
Where is the wonderful grass
And oldened seed? Alas!
I've tried to find them, but in vain.
Does the fairy cave still remain?
Do fairies often blow their phoenix flute
And play on broidered lute?
I sigh for the way is covered with moss,
No message comes from the stone gate, I'm at a loss.
The fairies would be hard to seek;
Would they lead me along the creek?

I turn my head, a boundless plain appears,
And petals shed like tears.
Lovers are easy to grow old. Have they heard
Where is the blue bird
To bring to them a word?
I would ask the fair maid
For whom the golden phoenix and green jade
Displaying their charm, are displayed.
When the lover wakes from his dream,
What's left is only fallen petals on the stream.

南柯子 | 徐默 绘 ▶
Song of a Dream | Painter: Xu Mo

南柯子

吴潜

池水凝新碧，栏花驻老红。有人独立画桥东，
手把一枝杨柳系春风。

鹊绊游丝坠，蜂拈落蕊空。秋千庭院小帘栊，
多少闲情闲绪雨声中。

Song of a Dream

Wu Qian

By pools of congealed green
Red flowers form a screen.
East of the painted bridge alone stands she,
Trying to bind spring breeze with sprigs of willow tree.

Magpies fly through gossamers light,
The bees alight on falling flowers in vain.
A swing hangs in the yard before the window bright.
How much sorrow and leisure she feels in the rain!

詩意圖
甲午秋月 健製

鹊桥仙

吴潜

扁舟昨泊，危亭孤啸，目断闲云千里。前山急雨过溪来，尽洗却、人间暑气。

暮鸦木末，落凫天际，都是一团秋意。痴儿騃女贺新凉，也不道、西风又起。

Immortals at the Magpie Bridge

Wu Qian

I moor my boat and then I croon
Beneath the high pavilion alone.
I stretch my eyes
To see for miles and miles clouds rise.
The hasty rain sweeps from the hills
Across the rills.

At dusk the crows perch on top of the trees;
From the horizon come the wild geese.
They bring the fresh autumnal air;
My children are fond of the fresh cool here and there.
They do not see the rise again of the west breeze.

山花子 | 何曦 绘 ▶
Song of Mountain Flowers | Painter: He Xi

劉辰翁
山花子詞意
何兮寫

山花子

刘辰翁

此处情怀欲问天，相期相就复何年。行过章江三十里，泪依然。

早宿半程芳草路，犹寒欲雨暮春天。小小桃花三两处，得人怜。

Song of Mountain Flowers

Liu Chenweng

Ask Heaven what I feel while parting here.
When may we meet again? Oh, in which year?
Thirty miles after the river disappears,
Still I'm in tears.

I take early rest by the grassy lane;
Still cold in late spring, I fear it will rain.
Two or three small flowers on the peach tree
Win my sympathy.

踏莎行　雨中观海棠 | 洪健 绘 ▶
Treading on Grass | Painter: Hong Jian

雨中觀海棠
甲午初秋於海上

踏莎行 | 雨中观海棠

刘辰翁

命薄佳人，情钟我辈。海棠开后心如碎。斜风细雨不曾晴，倚阑滴尽胭脂泪。

恨不能开，开时又背。春寒只了房栊闭。待他晴后得君来，无言掩帐羞憔悴。

Treading on Grass

Crabapple Flowers Viewed in Rain

Liu Chenweng

Ill-fated beauty in view,
How can I not fall in love with you?
I'm broken-hearted to see you fade.
In wind and rain fine day's no more;
You've shed all rouged tears by the balustrade.

To my regret you are not in full bloom
When you're in bloom, I fall in gloom.
For spring is cold and I must shut the door.
When the day's fine, I see you sigh,
Wordless, veiled by the screen, languid and shy.

鹊桥仙 | 鲍莺 绘 ▶
Immortals at the Magpie Bridge | Painter: Bao Ying

鹊桥仙

刘辰翁

天香吹下，烟霏成路。
飒飒神光暗度。
桥边犹记泛槎人，看赤岸、苔痕如古。

长空皓月，小风斜露。
寂寞江头独步。
人间何处得飘然，归梦入、梨花春雨。

Immortals at the Magpie Bridge

Liu Chenweng

Who blows celestial fragrance down
From misty Milky Way?
Who sheds divine light on my birthday?
I seem to see the Cowherd Star on the red shore,
Where moss grows as of yore.

But in the endless sky the moon is bright;
The dew is slight and the breeze light.
By riverside I stroll in lonely gown.
Where can I be carefree?
A dream of pear blossoms in tears haunts me.

花犯　水仙花 | 张雷平 绘 ▶
Invaded by Flowers | Painter: Zhang Leiping

仙葩
甲午冬月雷平畫於海上

花犯｜水仙花

周密

楚江湄，湘娥乍见，无言洒清泪。淡然春意。
空独倚东风，芳思谁寄。凌波路、冷秋无际，
香云随步起。谩记得、汉宫仙掌，亭亭明月底。

冰弦写怨更多情，骚人恨，枉赋芳兰幽芷。
春思远，谁叹赏、国香风味。相将共、岁寒
伴侣，小窗静，沉烟熏翠袂。幽梦觉，涓涓
清露，一枝灯影里。

Invaded by Flowers

To the Daffodil

Zhou Mi

By the southern rivershore
Like the princess you appear;
Silent, you shed tear on tear.
You care for spring no more,
In vain on eastern breeze you lean.
To whom will you send fragrance green?
You seem to tread on waves to hear cold autumn's sighs;
After your steps fragrant clouds rise,
To what avail should you
Recall the fairy with a plate of dew,
Who stands fair and bright in the moonlight?

The icy strings reveal the grief of lovesick heart.
The poet regrets to have sung of orchids and grass,
But keep you apart.
Your vernal thoughts go far away.
Who would enjoy the fragrance of bygone days?
Why not share with me the quiet window you've seen,
Where incense perfumes your sleeves green?
Awake from my sweet dream, alas!
I find by candlelight a part of you
Steeped in clear dew.

闻鹊喜 | 吴山观涛

周密

天水碧，染就一江秋色。鳌戴雪山龙起蛰，快风吹海立。

数点烟鬟青滴，一杼霞绡红湿，白鸟明边帆影直，隔江闻夜笛。

Glad to Hear Magpies

Zhou Mi

The sky with water blends,
The river dyed in autumn hues extends.
Snow-crowned hills and dragons rise from the deep;
Swift wind blows the sea up like a wall steep.

Blue dots seem to drip from mist-veiled hills,
The rainbow clouds redden the sky like grills.
Far away white birds mingle with sails white,
Beyond the stream we hear a flute at night.

◀ 闻鹊喜　吴山观涛 | 车鹏飞 绘
Glad to Hear Magpies | Painter: Che Pengfei

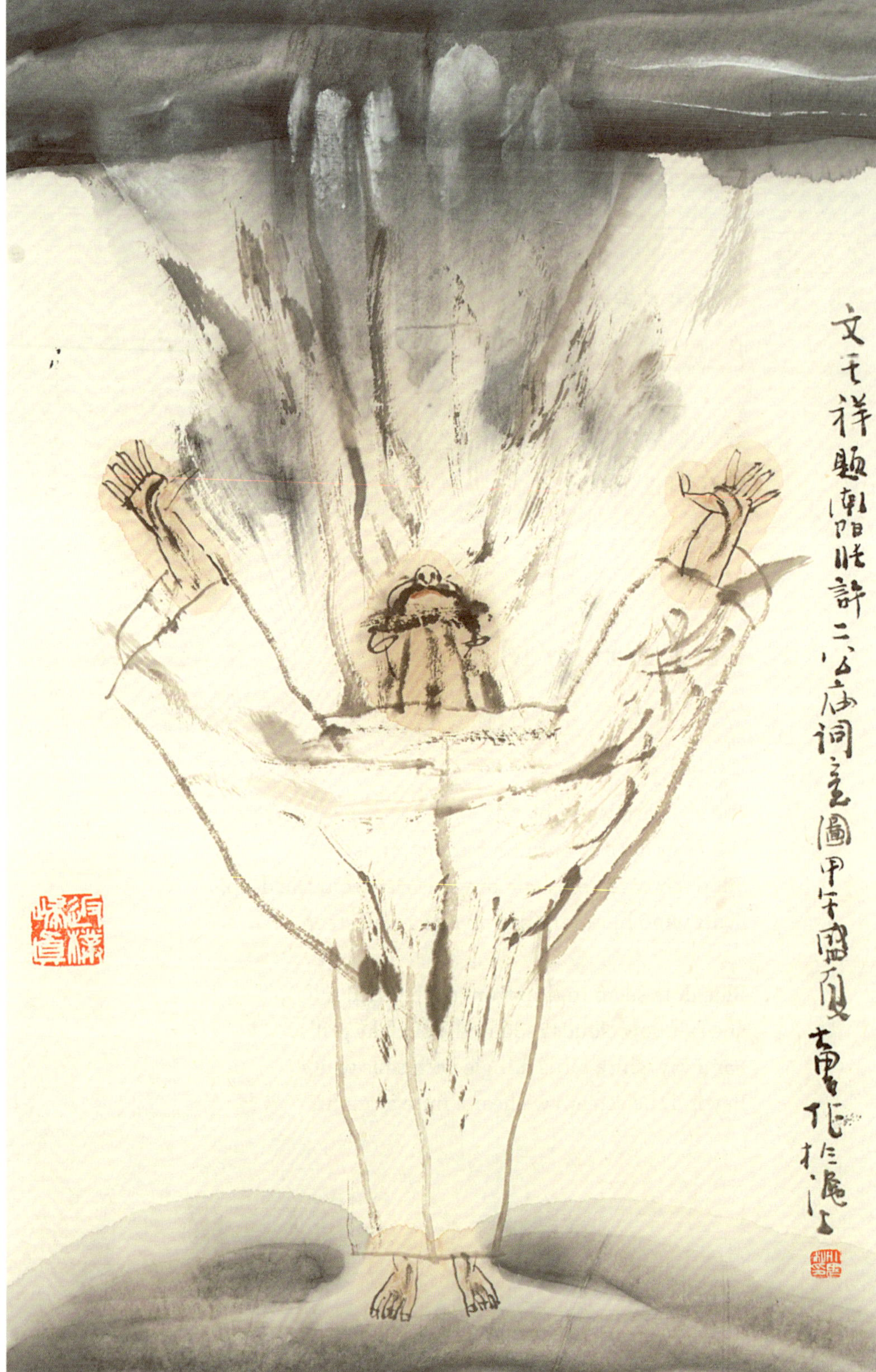
文天祥題潮陽張許二公廟詞意圖
甲午盛夏
作於滬上

沁园春｜题潮阳张许二公庙

文天祥

为子死孝，为臣死忠，死又何妨。自光岳气分，士无全节；君臣义缺，谁负刚肠。骂贼张巡，爱君许远，留取声名万古香。后来者，无二公之操，百炼之钢。

人生翕歘云亡。好烈烈轰轰做一场。使当时卖国，甘心降虏，受人唾骂，安得流芳。古庙幽沉，仪容俨雅，枯木寒鸦几夕阳。邮亭下，有奸雄过此，仔细思量。

◀ 沁园春 题潮阳张许二公庙｜施大畏 绘
Spring in a Pleasure Garden | Painter: Shi Dawei

Spring in a Pleasure Garden

Written in the Temple of Zhang Xun and Xu Yuan

Wen Tianxiang

If sons should die for filial piety
And ministers for loyalty,
What matters for us to be dead?
Our sacred land is torn in shreds,
No patriot could feel at ease,
Have loyal subjects done what they ought to?
How could my righteous wrath appease?
Zhang Xun, whom the rebels could not subdue,
And Xu Yuan were loyal to the crown;
They've left an undying renown.
Those who come after them should feel
The lack of their loyal zeal,
And they should be hardened into steel.

Life will soon pass away like a flickering flame;
A man should work, shine or rain,
With all his might and main.
If Zhang and Xu had fallen to the foe,
They would have borne the blame,
And down in history their names could never go.
Their temple gloomy at the forest's side,
Their statues, awe-inspiring, dignified,
How many times have they been worshipped when crows fly
Over old trees and the setting sun kindles the sky!
Should a traitor pass by,
Let him open his eye!

甘州　寄李筠房｜朱敏 绘 ▶
Song of Ganzhou｜Painter: Zhu Min

望渭渭一水隐芙蓉

甘州｜寄李筠房

张炎

望涓涓一水隐芙蓉，几被暮云遮。正凭高送目，西风断雁，残月平沙。未觉丹枫尽老，摇落已堪嗟。无避秋声处，愁满天涯。

一自盟鸥别后，甚酒瓢诗锦，轻误年华。料荷衣初暖，不忍负烟霞。记前度、翦灯一笑，再相逢、知在那人家。空山远，白云休赠，只赠梅花。

Song of Ganzhou

To a Friend

Zhang Yan

See lotus in bloom
On mist-veiled water loom!
I climb up high and gaze afar on the wild geese
Under the waning moon over the beach in west breeze.
I'm grieved for maples grown old
Have shed all red leaves cold.
Where can I not hear autumn sigh?
Grief brims over the end of the sky.

Since you left me, I've spent my years in verse and wine;
Clad in lotus, could you leave rainbow cloud so fine?
Last time we met, we laughed by candlelight;
Meeting again, can we enjoy the same delight?
Your mountain's bare and far away from my bower.
Do not bring me clouds white
But the cold-proof mume flower!

何兮

解连环｜孤雁

张炎

楚江空晚。怅离群万里，恍然惊散。自顾影、
欲下寒塘，正沙净草枯，水平天远。写不成书，
只寄得、相思一点。料因循误了，残毡拥雪，
故人心眼。

谁怜旅愁荏苒。谩长门夜悄，锦筝弹怨。想伴侣、
犹宿芦花，也曾念春前，去程应转。暮雨相呼，
怕蓦地、玉关重见。未羞他、双燕归来，画帘半卷。

◀ 解连环　孤雁｜何曦 绘
Double Rings Unchained | Painter: He Xi

Double Rings Unchained

Zhang Yan

Over the southern stream at the close of the day,
Suddenly startled, you go astray
And from the row in flight you're miles away.
You gaze at your own image in the sandy pool
And would alight 'mid withered grass by water cool.
Alone in the vast sky you cannot form a row,
So like a dot of yearning you should go.
How can you not delay
The message of the envoy eating wool
Mixed with snow!
Who would pity your loneliness?

The queen deserted, companionless,
At quiet night in Palace of Long Gate
Might play pitiful tunes on zither's string.
You may think of flowering reeds where rests your mate,
Who should come back before next spring.
What if you meet at Gate of Jade again,
Calling each other in the evening rain!
Then you won't envy swallows in pair,
Flitting by half unrolled curtain of the fair.

摸鱼子　高爱山隐居 | 车鹏飞 绘 ▶
Groping for Fish | Painter: Che Pengfei

摸鱼子｜高爱山隐居

张炎

爱吾庐、傍湖千顷，苍茫一片清润。晴岚暖翠融融处，花影倒窥天镜。沙浦迥。看野水涵波，隔柳横孤艇。眠鸥未醒。甚占得莼乡，都无人见，斜照起春暝。

还重省。岂料山中秦晋，桃源今度难认。林间即是长生路，一笑原非捷径。深更静。待散发吹箫，跨鹤天风冷。凭高露饮。正碧落尘空，光摇半壁，月在万松顶。

Groping for Fish

Hermitage in Mount High Love

Zhang Yan

I love my cot by the lakeside
So fair and wide,
A vast expanse so vague and clear.
On fine days the far-flung hills warm appear,
With flowers reflected in the mirror of the skies.
The sand beach far away, I seem
To see the rippling water beam,
Under the willow trees a lonely boat lies.
The gulls asleep, not yet awake,
Unseen in my native village by the lake.
The setting sun would bring
Twilight to spring.

I meditate:
Who can anticipate
Even Peach Blossom Land
Will witness dynasties fall or stand?
The pathway in the woods will lead to a long life.
I laugh, for it is not a shortcut to win in strife.
It's calm when deep is night,
I would play on my flute with loosened hair
And ride my crane to brave the cold wind in my flight.
I would drink dew on high
And waft in the air.
The moon atop the pines sheds its light
Over the conquered land far and nigh.

水龙吟｜白莲

张炎

仙人掌上芙蓉，涓涓犹滴金盘露。轻装照水，
纤裳玉立，飘飘似舞。几度销凝，满湖烟月，
一汀鸥鹭。记小舟夜悄，波明香远，浑不见、
花开处。

应是浣纱人妒。褪红衣、被谁轻误。闲情淡雅，
冶姿清润，凭娇待语。隔浦相逢，偶然倾盖，
似传心素。怕湘皋珮解，绿云十里，卷西风去。

◀ 水龙吟 白莲｜陈家泠 绘
Water Dragon Chant | Painter: Chen Jialing

Water Dragon Chant

To the White Lotus

Zhang Yan

The lotus in the fairy's band
Drips drops of dew on golden tray.
Mirrored on water, your light dress aglow,
Like jade in a fine robe you stand
As a dancer you swing and sway.
From time to time you fade and blow,
When the lake is veiled in mist or steeped in moonlight,
And gulls and herons perch on the sand.
Remember my leaflike boat in a quiet night
On clear waves where fragrance spreads far,
White dressed I cannot find where you are.

Even the beauty should envy you,
When you take your rosy dress off.
Who would not fall with you in love?
You are elegant at leisure
Or charming with pleasure.
You fascinate as if you would speak anew.
I see you in the lake in view:
Sometimes you lean apart
As if you would open your heart,
But when the west wind blows, I'm afraid,
With your cloudlike green leaves you would fade.

绮罗香　红叶 | 何曦 绘 ▶
Fragrance of Silk Brocade | Painter: He Xi

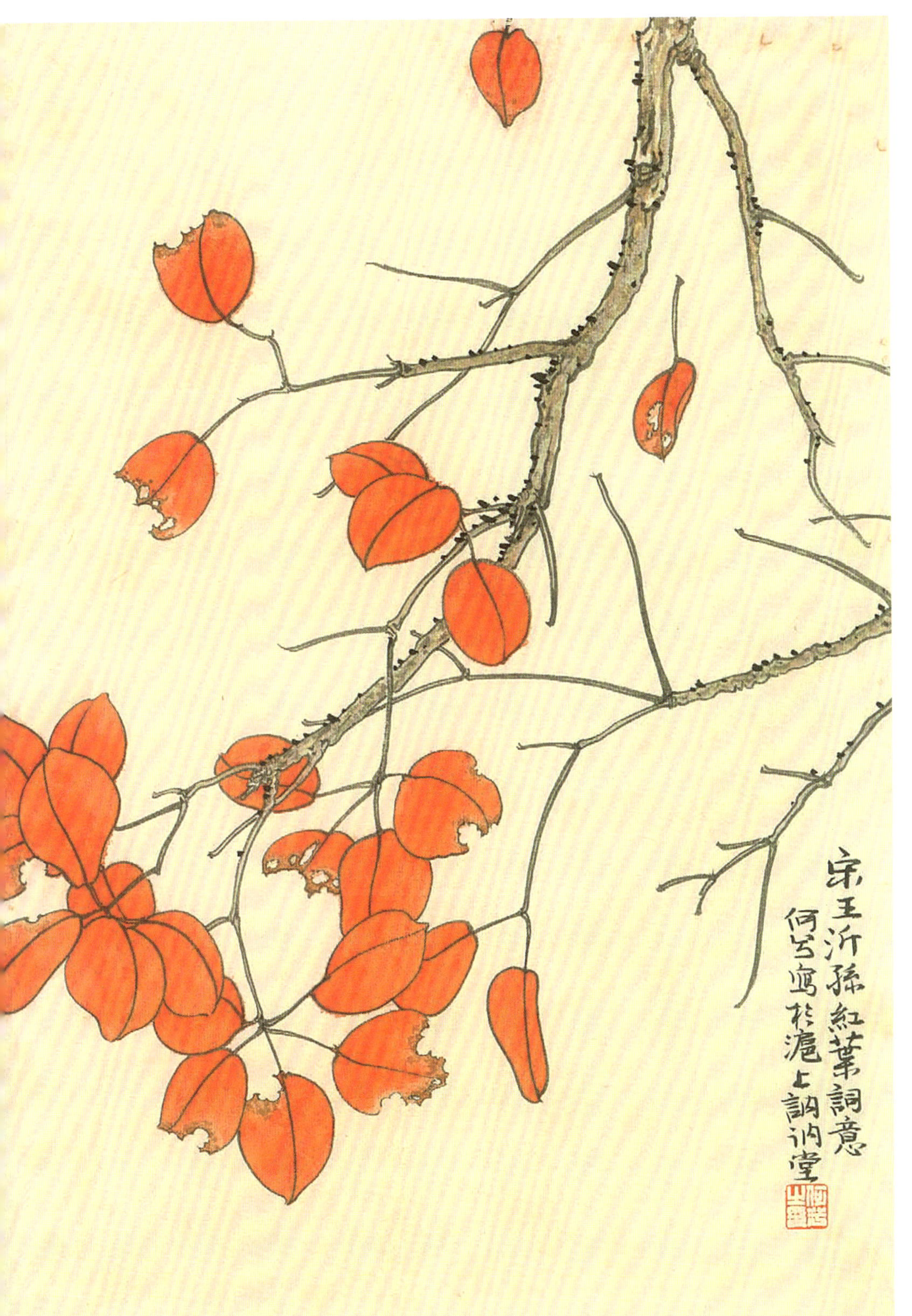
宋王沂孫紅葉詞意

绮罗香｜红叶

王沂孙

玉杵余丹，金刀剩彩，重染吴江孤树。几点朱铅，几度怨啼秋暮。惊旧梦、绿鬓轻凋，诉新恨、绛唇微注。最堪怜，同拂新霜，绣蓉一镜晚妆妒。

千林摇落渐少，何事西风老色，争妍如许。二月残花，空误小车山路。重认取、流水荒沟，怕犹有、寄情芳语。但凄凉、秋苑斜阳，冷枝留醉舞。

Fragrance of Silk Brocade

Red Leaves

Wang Yisun

In remnants of elixir red
And colored silken thread,
The riverside lonely tree's dyed.
A few rouged drops appear
Like late autumn's bloody tear.
Awake from dreams of old again,
Your green color fades and drips.
Of new grief you complain,
Biting your rouged lips.
We deplore all the more,
Though you are lost in frost,
The lotus looking down
On water envy your evening gown.

Shed down from wood to wood, fewer you grow.
Why should you vie in the west wind with evening glow?
Redder than spring flowers new,
More cabs would come along the path for you.
See close again
If on the water of the dike
There is a leaf looking alike
With love hidden in vain.
How sad and drear to see
In autumn garden you have left no trace.
The slanting sun shines only on cold dancing tree
With drunken face!

齐天乐｜蝉

王沂孙

一襟余恨宫魂断，年年翠阴庭树。乍咽凉柯，
还移暗叶，重把离愁深诉。西窗过雨。怪瑶珮
流空，玉筝调柱。镜暗妆残，为谁娇鬓尚如许。

铜仙铅泪似洗，叹携盘去远，难贮零露。病翼
惊秋，枯形阅世，消得斜阳几度。余音更苦。
甚独抱清商，顿成凄楚。谩想熏风，柳丝千万缕。

◀ 齐天乐　蝉｜庞飞 绘
A Skyful of Joy | Painter: Pang Fei

A Skyful of Joy

The Cicada

Wang Yisun

The cicada transformed form the wronged Queen of Qi
Pours out her broken heart from year to year on the tree.
It sobs now on cold twig and now on darkened leaves;
Again and again
It laments her death and grieves.
When the west window's swept by rain,
It sings in the air as her jasper pendant rings
Or her fair fingers play on zither's stings.
No longer black is now her mirrored hair;
I ask for whom its wings should still be black and fair.

The golden statue steeped in tears of lead
Was carried far away with plate in days of old.
Where can the cicada find dew on which it fed?
Its sickly wings are afraid of autumn cold
And its abandoned form has witnessed rise and fall.
How many sunsets can it still endure?
Its last song is saddest of all.
Why should it sing alone on high and pure.
And suddenly appear
So sad and drear?
Can it forget the summer breeze
When waved thousands of twigs of willow trees?

水龙吟　落叶 | 庞飞 绘 ▶
Water Dragon Chant | Painter: Pang Fei

水龙吟｜落叶

王沂孙

晓霜初著青林，望中故国凄凉早。萧萧渐积，
纷纷犹坠，门荒径悄。渭水风生，洞庭波起，
几番秋杪。想重厓半没，千峰尽出，山中路，
无人到。

前度题红杳杳，溯宫沟、暗流空绕。啼螀未歇，
飞鸿欲过，此时怀抱。乱影翻窗，碎声敲砌，
愁人多少。望吾庐甚处，只应今夜，满庭谁扫。

Water Dragon Chant

To Fallen Leaves

Wang Yisun

The green forest is lost in morning frost;
I think my homeland should look sad and drear.
Shower by shower you pile up high,
Leaves on leaves fall and sigh,
On the lane or before the door.
On the stream the breeze blows;
In the lake the waves roar,
Deeper and deeper autumn grows.
You cover half the hills high and low,
Bare peaks appear,
On mountain path few come and go.

No more verse on red leaf flows
From palace dike down
To wind around an empty town.
Cicadas trill without cease,
High up fly the wild geese,
They seem to know how my heart sighs.
How much it grieves
To see the shadow of falling leaves
And hear the sound when they scratch the ground.
I stretch my eyes
To see leaves cover my cot before the day.
Who will sweep them away?

词作者简介

曹冠（生卒年不详）
字宗臣，号双溪，东阳（今属浙江）人。有《燕喜词》。

曹组（生卒年不详）
字元宠，颍昌（今河南许昌）人。

陈东甫（生卒年不详）
吴兴（今属浙江）人。存词三首。

高观国（生卒年不详）
字宾王，山阴（今浙江绍兴）人。有《竹屋痴语》。

蒋捷（生卒年不详）
字胜欲，号竹山，阳羡（今江苏宜兴）人。宋末进士。入元隐居不仕。学者称竹山先生。词语言通俗，音节谐畅，风格多变化。有《竹山词》。

乐婉（生卒年不详）
宋代杭州妓，为施酒监所悦。

张辑（生卒年不详）
字宗瑞，鄱阳（今江西鄱阳县）人。有《沁园春》。

潘阆（?—1009）
字梦空，号逍遥子，大名（今属河北）人。至道间召对，赐进士及第。官至滁州参军。工诗词，名重一时。有《逍遥集》，今仅存《酒泉子》十首。

柳永（?—约1053）

原名三变，字景庄；后改名永，字耆卿，排行第七，崇安（今福建武夷山）人。景祐进士。官屯田员外郎。世称柳七、柳屯田。创作慢词独多。铺叙刻画，情景交融，语言通俗，音律谐婉。有《乐章集》。

张先（990—1078）

字子野，乌程（今浙江湖州）人。天圣进士。官至都官郎中。词风清婉，语言工巧。有《张子野词》。

晏殊（991—1055）

字同叔，抚州临川（今属江西）人。景德中赐同进士出身。官至同中书门下平章事兼枢密使。其词擅长小令，语言婉丽。仅存《珠玉词》及清人所辑《晏元献遗文》。

张昪（992—1077）

字杲卿，韩城（今陕西）人。进士出身。官至参知政事。仅存词四首。

宋祁（998—1061）

字子京，安州安陆（今湖北安陆）人。天圣二年进士。官翰林学士、史馆修撰。诗词语言工丽。有《玉楼春》。

欧阳修（1007—1072）

字永叔，号醉翁、六一居士，吉州吉水（今属江西）人。天圣进士。官至翰林学士、枢密副使、参知政事。其词婉丽，承袭南唐余风。有《欧阳文忠公文集》。

王安石（1021—1086）

字介甫，号半山，抚州临川（今属江西）人。庆历进士。词风格高峻。有文集《王文公文集》《临川先生文集》。

王安国（1028—1074）

字平甫，临川（今江西抚州）人。世称王安礼、王安国、王雱为“临川三王”。

李之仪（约1035—1117）

字端叔，号姑溪居士，沧州无棣（今属山东）人。神宗时进士。历官提举河东常平。有《姑溪居士文集》《姑溪词》。

苏轼（1037—1101）

字子瞻，号东坡居士，眉州眉山（今属四川乐山）人。嘉祐进士。官至礼部尚书。词开豪放一派，对后世很有影响。有《东坡七集》和《东坡乐府》。

晏几道（1038—1110）

字叔原，号小山，抚州临川（今属江西）人。晏殊第七子。历任颍昌府许田镇监、乾宁军通判、开封府判官等。有《小山词》。

黄庭坚（1045—1105）

字鲁直，号山谷道人、涪翁，洪州分宁（今江西修水）人。治平进士。曾任国子监教授、国史编修官等职。有《山谷集》《山谷精华录》《山谷琴趣外篇》。

王诜（1048—1104）

字晋卿，太原（今属山西）人。尚蜀国公主，官驸马都尉。善诗词、书法，尤工山水。存世山水作品有《烟江叠嶂》《渔村小雪》等。

秦观（1049—1100）

字少游、太虚，号淮海居士，高邮（今属江苏）人。元丰进士。曾任太学博士，兼国史院编修官等职。词风格委婉含蓄，清丽雅淡。有《淮海集》《淮海居士长短句》。

贺铸（1052—1125）

字方回，号庆湖遗老，卫州（今河南卫辉）人，祖籍山阴（今浙江绍兴）。曾任泗州、太平州通判。其词风格多样，善于锤炼字句。有《东山词》《贺方回词》。

晁补之（1053—1110）

字无咎，号归来子，济州巨野（今属山东）人。元丰进士。曾任礼部郎中、国史编修官、知河中府等职。有《鸡肋集》《晁氏琴趣外篇》。

周邦彦（1056—1121）

字美成，号清真居士，钱塘（今浙江杭州）人。历官太学正、知溧水县、国子监主簿。格律谨严，语言典丽精雅，长调尤善铺叙。有《片玉集》。

叶梦得（1077—1148）
字少蕴，号肖翁、石林居士，原籍吴县（今属江苏）。绍圣进士。曾任江东安抚制置大使，兼知建康府、行宫留守。有《建康集》《石林词》《石林词话》《避暑录话》《石林燕语》等。

朱敦儒（1081—1159）
字希真，号岩壑老人，洛阳（今属河南）人。曾任两浙东路提点刑狱。词语言清畅俚俗。有词集《樵歌》。

李清照（1084—约1151）
号易安居士，齐州章丘（今属山东）人。词善用白描手法，自辟途径，语言清丽。后人有《漱玉词》辑本，今人有《李清照集校注》。

陈与义（1090—1139）
字去非，号简斋，洛阳（今属河南）人。官至参知政事。有《简斋集》和《无住词》。

岳飞（1103—1142）
字鹏举，相州汤阴（今属河南）人。曾任清远军节度使、枢密副使。诗词文皆慷慨激昂。有《岳武穆遗文》（一作《岳忠武王文集》）。

陆游（1125—1210）
字务观，号放翁，越州山阴（今浙江绍兴）人。孝宗时赐进士出身。曾任镇江、隆兴通判，后官至宝章阁待制。有《剑南诗稿》《渭南文集》《放翁词》《南唐书》《老学庵笔记》等。

杨万里（1127—1206）
字廷秀，学者称诚斋先生，吉水（今属江西）人。绍兴进士。官至宝谟阁学士。有《诚斋乐府》。

张孝祥（1132—1170）
字安国，号于湖居士，乌江（今安徽和县）人。绍兴进士。官荆南、湖北安抚使。词风格豪迈。有《于湖居士文集》《于湖词》。

辛弃疾（1140—1207）
字幼安，号稼轩，历城（今山东济南）人。历任湖北、江西、湖南、福建、浙东安抚使等职。词艺术风格多样，而以豪放为主。热情洋溢，慷慨悲壮，笔力雄厚，与苏轼并称为“苏辛”。有《稼轩长短句》，今人辑有《辛稼轩诗文钞存》。

杨炎正（1145—？）
字济翁，庐陵（今江西吉安）人。庆元进士。曾任大理司直。有词集《西樵语业》。

刘过（1154—1206）
字改之，号龙洲道人，吉州太和（今江西泰和）人。有《龙洲集》《龙洲词》。

汪莘（1155—？）
字叔耕，自号方壶居士，休宁（今属安徽）人。

史达祖（1163？—1220？）
字邦卿，号梅溪，汴（今河南开封）人。嘉泰、开禧间为韩侂胄堂吏，掌文书。其词多抒写闲情逸致，描写细腻工巧。有《梅溪词》。

戴复古（1167—？）
字式之，号石屏，台州黄岩（今属浙江台州）人。词风格雄放。有《石屏诗集》《石屏词》。

曹豳（1170—1249）
字西士，号东亩，一作东猷，温州瑞安（今属浙江）人。嘉泰进士。历任安吉州教授、秘书丞兼仓部郎官、左司谏等官。存词二首。

葛长庚（1194—1229）
名白玉蟾，字如晦，又字白叟，号海琼子。琼州（今海南琼山）人，一说福建闽清人。尝封为紫清真人，世称紫清先生。著有《玉隆集》《上清集》《武夷集》等。

吴潜（1195—1262）
字毅夫，号履斋，宣州宁国（今属安徽）人。嘉定进士。官至右丞相。明梅鼎祚辑有《履斋遗集》，另有词集《履斋诗余》。

刘辰翁（1232—1297）

字会孟，号须溪，吉州庐陵（今江西吉安）人。景定进士。曾任濂溪书院院长、临安府学教授。明人辑有《须溪记钞》，清人辑有《须溪集》，又有《须溪词》。

周密（1232—约1298）

字公谨，号草窗、蘋州、四水潜夫等，原籍济南，后为吴兴（今浙江湖州）人。其词讲求格律，语意蕴藉。有词集《蘋州渔笛谱》（又名《草窗词》）。

文天祥（1236—1283）

字履善，一字宋瑞，号文山，吉州吉水（今属江西）人。宝祐进士。官至右丞相。所作《正气歌》为世所传诵。有《文山先生全集》。

张炎（1248—1314后）

字叔夏，号玉田、乐笑翁，临安（今浙江杭州）人。词用字工巧，追求典雅，尤长于咏物词。有词集《山中白云》和词论《词源》。

王沂孙（约1250—约1290）

字圣与，号碧山、中仙、玉笥山人，会稽（今浙江绍兴）人。曾任庆元路学正。有《花外集》，又名《碧山乐府》。

参考文献

《辞海》编辑委员会编辑　《辞海》（彩图本）〔M〕
1999年　上海辞书出版社

胡云翼选注　《宋词选》〔M〕
1978年　上海古籍出版社

唐圭璋主编　《唐宋词鉴赏辞典》〔M〕
1986年　江苏古籍出版社

About the Lyricists

Cao Guan

Cao Guan, also known as Zongchen (courtesy name), and Shuangxi (literary name), was a native of Dongyang (in present-day Zhejiang Province). His lyrics are collected in the *Lyrics of Yanxi*.

Cao Zu

Cao Zu, also known as Yuanchong (courtesy name), was a native of Yingchang (present-day Xuchang City, Henan Province).

Chen Dongfu

Chen Dongfu was a native of Wuxing (in present-day Zhejiang Province). Only three lyrics of his have come down to us.

Gao Guanguo

Gao Guanguo, also known as Binwang (courtesy name), was a native of Shanyin (present-day Shaoxing City, Zhejiang Province). His lyrics are collected in the *Zhuwu Chiyu*.

Jiang Jie

Jiang Jie, also known as Shengyu (courtesy name), and Zhushan (literary name), was a native of Yangxian (present-day Yixing City, Jiangsu Province). He passed the imperial examination in the late Song Dynasty, but gave up his official position when Song Dynasty was replaced by Yuan and lived in seclusion ever since. He is also called Sir Zhushan by scholars. His lyrics are easy to read, with a variety of styles and harmoniously-organized syllables. His lyrics are compiled into the *Lyrics of Zhushan*.

Le Wan

Le Wan was a famous courtesan in Hangzhou in the Song Dynasty. She was adored by the lyrics writer Shi Jiujian.

Zhang Ji

Zhang Ji, also known as Zongrui (courtesy name), was a native of Poyang (present-day Poyang County, Jiangxi Province). His lyrics are collected in the *Spring in a Pleasure Garden*.

Pan Lang

Pan Lang (?—1009), also known as Mengkong (courtesy name), and Xiaoyaozi (literary name), was a native of Daming (in present-day Hebei Province). In 995, he was summoned by the Emperor Taizong of Song to take the imperial examination, which he passed successfully, and since then worked his way up to military staff officer in Chuzhou. He gained considerable fame among his contemporaries for his poetry and lyrics. His lyrics are compiled into the *Xiaoyao Ji*, and only ten of them named "Jiuquanzi" (Fountain of Wine) have come down to us.

Liu Yong

Liu Yong (?—c.1053), once known as Sanbian, or Jingzhuang (courtesy name), renamed himself as Yong, or Qiqing (courtesy name) later in his life. A native of Chong'an (present-day Wuyishan City, Fujian Province), he ranked seventh in his family. He passed the imperial examination during the Jingyou period in the Song Dynasty and was appointed as *Tuntian Yuanwailang* ("deputy officer in charge of reclaiming wasteland"). Therefore, he was also called Liu Qi (Qi means seven) or Liu Tuntian. He was especially good at creating *manci*, a type of Song lyrics accompanied by slow musical rhythm. Due to their harmonious and mild rhyme, his lyrics are easy to read, with the scenery depicted and the emotions expressed in perfect harmony. His lyrics are collected in the *Yuezhang Ji*.

Zhang Xian

Zhang Xian (990—1078), also known as Ziye (courtesy name), was a native of Wucheng (present-day Huzhou City, Zhejiang Province). He passed the imperial examination during the Tiansheng period in the Song Dynasty, and served as the official in charge of rectifying malpractices in the capital city. His lyrics are mild, tactful and exquisite. His lyrics are collected in the *Lyrics of Zhang Ziye*.

Yan Shu

Yan Shu (991—1055), also named Tongshu (courtesy name), was a native of Linchuan, Fuzhou (in present-day Jiangxi Province). He passed the imperial examination during the Jingde period in the Song Dynasty, and the highest position he held in the government was chancellor in charge of both government and military affairs. He was good at *xiaoling*, a type of Song lyrics composed of no more than 58 characters, and his language are beautiful and mild. The only existing lyrics of his are collected in the *Lyrics of Zhuyu* and the *Lost Writings of Yan Yuanxian*, the latter compiled by people in Qing Dynasty.

Zhang Bian

Zhang Bian (992—1077), also known as Gaoqing (courtesy name), was a native of Hancheng (present-day Shaanxi Province). He passed the imperial examination, and served as manager of affairs with the Secretariat-Chancellery. Only four of his lyrics have come down to us.

Song Qi

Song Qi (998—1061), also known as Zijing (courtesy name), was a native of Anlu in Anzhou (present-day Anlu City, Hubei Province). He passed the imperial examination in the second year of Tiansheng period in the Song Dynasty. He worked as imperial secretariat, and an editor who compiled national history. Featured with refined and rhetorical language, his lyrics are compiled into *Yulouchun*.

Ouyang Xiu

Ouyang Xiu (1007—1072), also known as Yongshu (courtesy name), and Zuiweng or Liuyi Jushi (literary name), was native to Jishui, Jizhou (in present-day Jiangxi Province). He passed the imperial examination in the second year of the Tiansheng period in the Song Dynasty, and worked as imperial secretariat, vice director in the army and manager of affairs with the Secretariat-Chancellery. His lyrics followed the graceful style of the Southern Tang Dynasty and are included in the *Collection of Ouyang Wenzhonggong's Works*.

Wang Anshi

Wang Anshi (1021—1086), also named Jiefu (courtesy name), and Banshan (literary name), was a native of Linchuan, Fuzhou (in present-day Jiangxi Province). He passed the imperial examination during the Qingli period in the Song Dynasty. His lyrics are featured with uplifting and bold style, which are included in the *Collection of Wang Wengong's Works* and *Collection of Linchuan Xiansheng's Works.*

Wang Anguo

Wang Anguo (1028—1074), also known as Pingfu (courtesy name), was a native of Linchuan (present-day Fuzhou City, Jiangxi Province). He, together with Wang Anli and Wang Pang, are called "Three Wangs in Linchuan".

Li Zhiyi

Li Zhiyi (c.1035—1117), also known as Duanshu (courtesy name), and Guxi Jushi (literary name), was a native of Wudi, Cangzhou (in present-day Shandong Province). He passed the imperial examination during the Shenzong period in the Song Dynasty and served as a senior official in charge of farmland, water conservancy, etc. He authored the *Collection of Guxi Jushi's Works* and the *Lyrics of Guxi*.

Su Shi

Su Shi (1037—1101), also known as Zizhan (courtesy name), and Dongpo Jushi (literary name), was a native of Meishan, Meizhou (in present-day Leshan, Sichuan Province). He passed the imperial examination during the Jiayou period, and the highest position he held in the government was Minister of Rites. His lyrics, featured with bold style, have a great influence on later generations. His works are included in the *Dongpo Qiji* and the *Dongpo Yuefu*.

Yan Jidao

Yan Jidao (1038—1110), also named Shuyuan (courtesy name), and Xiaoshan (literary name), was a native of Linchuan, Fuzhou (in present-day Jiangxi Province). He was the seventh son of Yanshu. He once worked as the chief of Xutian Town in Yingchang Commandery, vice magistrate in Qianningjun, assistant to the chief local official in Kaifeng, etc. His lyrics are collected in the *Lyrics of Xiaoshan*.

Huang Tingjian

Huang Tingjian (1045—1105), also named Luzhi (courtesy name), and Shangu Daoren or Fuweng (literary name), was a native of Fenning, Hongzhou (present-day Xiushui County, Jiangxi Province). He passed the imperial examination in the Zhiping period. He once worked as an official at the Imperial Academy, and an editor who compiled national history. His works are included in the *Shangu Ji*, the *Shangu Jinghua Lu*, and the *Shangu Jinghua Waipian*.

Wang Shen

Wang Shen (1048—1104), also named Jin Qing (courtesy name), was a native of Taiyuan (in present-day Shanxi Province). He was chosen as the husband of the Princess of Shu, thus becoming the Emperor's son-in-law. He was good at composing poems and lyrics, as well as calligraphy, and he was especially skilled at landscape painting. His famous paintings that come down include the *Mist over the River with Mountains Surrounded*, the *Light Snow in a Fishing Village*, and others.

Qin Guan

Qin Guan (1049—1100), also named Shaoyou or Taixu (courtesy name), and Huaihai Jushi (literary name), was a native of Gaoyou (in present-day Jiangsu Province). He passed the imperial examination during the Yuanfeng period. He once worked as an official at the Imperial Academy and an editor who compiled national history, etc. His works, featured with mild and graceful style, are included in the *Huaihai Ji* and the *Huaihai Jushi Changduanju*.

He Zhu

He Zhu (1052—1125), also known as Fanghui (courtesy name), and Qinghu Yilao (literary name), was a native of Weizhou (present-day Weihui City, Henan Province). His ancestral home was in Shanyin (present-day Shaoxing City, Zhejiang Province). He once worked as the magistrate of Sizhou and Taiping commanderies. His lyrics, which are collected in the *Lyrics of Dongshan* and the *Lyrics of He Fanghui*, are of various styles and are featured with elaborate words and sentences.

Chao Buzhi

Chao Buzhi (1053—1110), also known as Wujiu (courtesy name), and Guilaizi (literary name), was a native of Juye, Jizhou (in present-day Shandong Province). He passed the imperial examination during the Yuanfeng Period. He once worked as a senior official in the Ministry of Rites, an editor who compiled national history, and magistrate of the Hezhong, etc. His works are collected in the *Jilei Ji* and *Chaoshi Qinqu Waipian*.

Zhou Bangyan

Zhou Bangyan (1056—1121), also known as Meicheng (courtesy name), and Qingzhen Jushi (literary name), was a native of Qiantang (present-day Hangzhou City, Zhejiang Province). He once worked in the Imperial College and the Imperial Academy. His lyrics are featured with careful rules and forms, graceful language, and he was good at narration when composing long tune. His works are collected in the *Pianyu Ji*.

Ye Mengde

Ye Mengde (1077—1148), also known as Shaoyun (courtesy name), and Xiaoweng or Shilin Jushi (literary name), was a native of Wuxian (in present-day Jiangsu Province). He passed the imperial examination during the Shaosheng period. He once worked as an official in charge of local administrative and military affairs in Jiangdong, magistrate of Jiankang, and others. His works are collected in the *Jiankang Ji*, the *Lyrics of Shilin*, the *Shilin Cihua*, the *Bishu Luhua*, the *Shilin Yanyu*, etc.

Zhu Dunru

Zhu Dunru (1081—1159), also known as Xizhen (courtesy name) and Yanhe Laoren (literary name), was a native of Luoyang (in present-day Henan Province). He once worked as an official in charge of prisoners. His works, featured with easy and refreshing style, are collected in the *Qiaoge*.

Li Qingzhao

Li Qingzhao (1084-c.1151), whose literary name is Yi'an Jushi, was a native of Zhangqiu, Qizhou (in present-day Shandong Province). With a simple and straightforward style, her works, with a unique and graceful style, were collected in the *Lyrics of Shuyu* by her later generations, and the work that passed down till now is known as the *Collation and Annotation of the Works of Li Qingzhao*.

Chen Yuyi

Chen Yuyi(1090—1139), also known as Qufei (courtesy name) and Jianzhai (literary name), was a native of Luoyang (in present-day Henan Province). He worked his way up to manager of affairs with the Secretariat-Chancellery. His works are collected in the *Jianzhai Ji* and the *Lyrics of Wuzhu*.

Yue Fei

Yue Fei (1103—1142), whose courtesy name is Pengju, was a native of Tangyin, Xiangzhou (in present-day Henan Province). He once worked as a military officer in the Qingyuan Army. His works, bold and impassioned, are collected in the *Yue Wumu Yiwen*.

Lu You

Lu You (1125—1210), also known as Wuguan (courtesy name), and Fangweng (literary name), was a native of Shanyin of Yuezhou (present-day Shaoxing City, Zhejiang Province). He passed the imperial examination during the Kaozong period, and he was unsuccessful in his official career. His works include the *Jiannan Shigao*, the *Weinan Wenji*, the *Lyrics of Fangweng*, the *Book of Southern Tang*, the *Laoxue'an Biji*, etc.

Yang Wanli

Yang Wanli (1127—1206), whose courtesy name is Tingxiu, was a native of Jishui (in present-day Jiangxi Province). He was also called Sir Chengzhai by scholars. He passed the imperial examination during the Shaoxing period and served a number of minor official posts in the Song Dynasty. His works are collected in the *Chengzhai Yuefu*.

Zhang Xiaoxiang

Zhang Xiaoxiang (1132—1170), also known as Anguo (courtesy name), and Yuhu Jushi (literary name), was a native of Wujiang (present-day Hexian County, Anhui Province). He passed the imperial examination during the Shaoxing period and was appointed commandant in Jingnan and Hubei. His lyrics, featured with bold style, are included in the *Collection of Yuhu Jushi's Works* and the *Lyrics of Yuhu*.

Xin Qiji

Xin Qiji (1140—1207), also known as You'an (courtesy name), and Jiaxuan (literary name), was a native of Licheng (present-day Jinan City, Shandong Province). He once worked as commandant in Hubei, Jiangxi, Hunan, Fujian and Zhedong. Bold and impassioned, his works displayed a variety of styles and are collected in the *Lyrics of Jiaxuan*. He, together with Su Shi, are called by people as "Su-Xin". And people today also edit a book named the *Xin Jiaxuan Shiwen Chaocun*.

Yang Yanzheng

Yang Yanzheng (1145—?), whose courtesy name is Jiweng, was a native of Luling (present-day Ji'an City, Jiangxi Province). He passed the imperial examination during the Qingyuan period. He once worked in the Court of Judicial Review. His works are collected in the *Xiqiao Yuye*.

Liu Guo

Liu Guo (1154—1206), also known as Gaizhi (courtesy name), and Longzhou Daoren (literary name), was a native of Taihe of Jizhou (present-day Taihe County, Jiangxi Province). His works are included in the *Longzhou Ji* and the *Lyrics of Longzhou*.

Wang Xin

Wang Xin (1155—?), also known as Shugeng (courtesy name), and Fanghu Jushi (literary name), was native to Xiuning (in present-day Anhui Province).

Shi Dazu

Shi Dazu (c.1163—c.1220), also known as Bangqing (courtesy name) and Meixi (literary name), was native to Bian (present-day Kaifeng City, Henan Province). He once worked as an assistant in charge of documents to Prime Minister Han Tuozhou in the mid Southern Song Dynasty. His lyrics, featured with elaborate style, mainly express a leisurely and carefree mood. His works are collected in the *Lyrics of Meixi*.

Dai Fugu

Dai Fugu (1167—?), also known as Shizhi (courtesy name), and Shiping (literary name), was a native of Huangyan, Taizhou (present-day Taizhou City, Zhejiang Province). His lyrics, featured with bold style, are included in the *Collections of Shiping's Poems* and the *Lyrics of Shiping*.

Cao Bin

Cao Bin (c.1170—c.1249?), also known as Xishi (courtesy name), and Dongmu or Dongyou (literary name), was native to Rui'an of Wenzhou (in present-day Zhejiang Province). He passed the imperial examination in the Jiatai period. He once worked as a senior official in charge of education in Anji Commandery, director of secretariat, attendant of storage department and others. Only two of his lyrics have been passed down.

Ge Changgeng

Ge Changgeng (1194—1229), named Bai Yuchan, was also called Ruhui or Baisou (courtesy name), and Haiqiongzi (literary name). He was said to be a native of Qiongzhou (present-day Qiongshan, Hainan Province), or Minqing of Fujian. He was given the title "Perfect Man of Ziqing" and was called Sir Ziqing. His works are included in the *Yulong Ji*, the *Shangqing Ji*, the *Wuyi Ji* and others.

Wu Qian

Wu Qian (1195—1262), also called Yifu (courtesy name), or Lvzhai (literary name), was native to Ningguo of Xuanzhou (in present-day Anhui Province). He passed the imperial examination during the Jiading period, and the highest position he held in the government was Right Prime Minister. His works are collected in the *Lost Writings of Lvzhai* (compiled by Mei Dingzuo in the Ming Dynasty) and the *Lvzhai Shiyu*.

Liu Chenweng

Liu Chenweng (1232—1297), also known as Huimeng (courtesy name) and Xuxi (literary name), was a native of Luling, Jizhou (present-day Ji'an City, Jiangxi Province). He passed the imperial examination during the Jingding period in the Southern Song Dynasty. He once worked as the dean of the Lianxi Academy and was a senior official in charge of education in Lin'an. His works are compiled into the *Xuxi Jichao* (by people in the Ming Dynasty), the *Xuxi Ji* (by people in the Qing Dynasty), and the *Lyrics of Xuxi*.

Zhou Mi

Zhou Mi (1232—c.1298) was also known as Gongjin (courtesy name), and Caochuang, Pingzhou, or Sishuiqianfu (literary name). His ancestral home was in Jinan, but he was a native of Wuxing (present-day Huzhou City, Zhejiang Province). His lyrics, strictly abided by the rules of classical poetic composition and featured with implicit words, are collected in the *Pingzhou Yudipu* (also named the *Lyrics of Caochuang*).

Wen Tianxiang

Wen Tianxiang (1236—1283), also known as Lvshan or Songrui (courtesy name), and Wenshan (literary name), was native to Jishui of Jizhou (in present-day Jiangxi Province). He passed the imperial examination during the Baoyou period in the Southern Song Dynasty, and the highest position he held in the government was Right Prime Minister. His poem the "Song of Righteousness" was widely known. His works are compiled into the *Collections of Sir Wenshan's Works*.

Zhang Yan

Zhang Yan (1248—?), also known as Shuxia (courtesy name), Yutian or Lexiaoweng (literary name), was native to Lin'an (present-day Hangzhou City, Zhejiang Province). His lyrics are featured with tactful and graceful style. He was especially good at composing lyrics chanting things. His works are collected in the *Cloud in the Mountain* and the *Ci Yuan*.

Wang Yisun

Wang Yisun (c.1250—c.1290), also known as Shengyu (courtesy name), and Bishan, Zhongxian or Yusi Shanren (literary name), was native to Kuaiji (present-day Shaoxing City, Zhejiang Province). He once worked as the director of education in Qingyuan Region. His works are compiled into the *Huawai Ji*, also named the *Bishan Yuefu*.

Bibliography

Ci Hai Editorial Board, *Ci Hai* (Illustrated Edition) 〔M〕
1999 Shanghai Lexicographical Publishing House

Hu Yunyi, *Selected Lyrics of the Song Dynasty* 〔M〕
1978 Shanghai Classics Publishing House

Tang Guizhang, *Dictionary for Appreciation of the Tang and Song Lyrics* 〔M〕
1986 Jiangsu Classics Publishing House

绘画作者简介

陈佩秋（女，1923 年生）

河南南阳人。毕业于国立艺术专科学校。上海中国画院画师，上海市文史研究馆馆员，中国美术家协会会员，上海市美术家协会荣誉顾问，上海中国画院顾问，上海大学美术学院兼职教授。现为上海书画院院长、海上印社社长。

林曦明（1926 年生）

浙江永嘉人。上海中国画院画师。上海市文史研究馆馆员，中国美术家协会会员，上海大学美术学院兼职教授。曾任中国剪纸学会名誉会长、上海剪纸学会会长。

陈家泠（1937 年生）

浙江杭州人。毕业于浙江美术学院。上海中国画院兼职画师，中国美术家协会会员，上海大学美术学院教授，中国国家画院研究员。

戴敦邦（1938 年生）

江苏镇江人。毕业于上海第一师范学校。上海中国画院兼职画师，中国美术家协会会员，上海交通大学教授。

张桂铭（1939 年—2014 年）

浙江绍兴人。毕业于浙江美术学院。上海中国画院兼职画师，中国美术家协会会员，中国国家画院研究员。曾任上海中国画院副院长、刘海粟美术馆执行馆长。

杨正新（1942 年生）

上海人。毕业于上海美术专科学校。上海中国画院画师，中国美术家协会会员，上海大学美术学院兼职教授。

萧海春（1944 年生）
江西丰城人。毕业于上海工艺美术学校。上海中国画院兼职画师，中国工艺美术大师，上海市美术家协会会员。

蔡天雄（1944 年生）
江苏无锡人。毕业于上海工艺美术学校。上海中国画院兼职画师，中国美术家协会会员。曾任上海工艺美术学校中国画研究室主任。

韩硕（1945 年生）
浙江杭州人。毕业于上海大学美术学院。上海中国画院画师。上海大学美术学院兼职教授。曾任上海中国画院副院长、中国美术家协会理事。现为上海中国画院艺委会主任、中国画学会副会长。

张雷平（女，1945 年生）
浙江乐清人。毕业于上海戏剧学院。上海中国画院画师，中国美术家协会会员，上海市美术家协会顾问。曾任上海市美术家协会副主席、上海中国画院副院长。

张培成（1948 年生）
江苏太仓人。上海中国画院兼职画师。中国美术家协会会员，上海大学美术学院兼职教授。曾任刘海粟美术馆执行馆长，现为上海市美术家协会副主席。

卢甫圣（1949 年生）
浙江东阳人。毕业于浙江美术学院。上海中国画院兼职画师，上海市文史研究馆馆员。现为中国美术家协会理事、上海市美术家协会副主席、中国美术学院兼职教授、上海书画出版社总编辑。

江宏（1949 年生）
上海人。上海中国画院兼职画师，上海市美术家协会理事。曾任上海书画院执行院长。

施大畏（1950 年生）
浙江湖州人。毕业于上海大学美术学院。上海大学美术学院兼职教授，全国政协委员。现为中国美术家协会副主席、上海市文联主席、上海市美术家协会主席、中国国家画院院委兼研究员、中华艺术宫馆长、上海中国画院院长。

车鹏飞（1951年生）

山东莱阳人。毕业于上海师范大学。上海中国画院画师，中国美术家协会会员，上海市美术家协会常务理事。曾任上海中国画院副院长。

朱新昌（1954年生）

浙江宁波人。毕业于上海师范大学。上海中国画院画师，中国美术家协会会员，上海市美术家协会理事。

马小娟（女，1955年生）

江苏南京人。毕业于浙江美术学院。上海中国画院画师，中国美术家协会会员，上海市美术家协会常务理事。现为上海中国画院教研室主任。

高云（1956年生）

江苏南京人。毕业于南京艺术学院。全国政协委员。现为中国美术家协会中国画艺委会副主任、中国画学会副会长、全国美术馆专委会副主任、中国国家画院院委兼研究员、中国艺术研究院中国画研究员、江苏省美术馆名誉馆长、江苏省文化厅副厅长。

陈向迅（1956年生）

浙江杭州人。毕业于浙江美术学院。中国美术家协会会员。曾任中国美术学院中国画系主任。现为中国美术学院学术委员会委员、中国画系教授、中国国家画院研究员。

朱敏（1956年生）

浙江新昌人。毕业于浙江美术学院。上海中国画院画师，上海市美术家协会理事。现为上海中国画院创研室副主任。

乐震文（1956年生）

浙江镇海人。上海中国画院兼职画师，中国美术家协会会员，上海市美术家协会理事。曾任上海大学美术学院中国画系主任。现为上海海事大学徐悲鸿艺术学院院长、上海书画院执行院长。

丁筱芳（1957年生）

浙江绍兴人。毕业于上海大学美术学院。上海中国画院画师，中国美术家协会会员，上海市美术家协会理事。

汪家芳（1959 年生）

上海嘉定人。毕业于华东师范大学。上海中国画院兼职画师，中国美术家协会会员，上海市美术家协会常务理事。

何曦（1960 年生）

浙江嘉兴人。毕业于浙江美术学院。上海中国画院画师，中国美术家协会会员，上海市美术家协会理事。现为上海中国画院创研室主任。

徐默（1960 年生）

福建福州人。毕业于浙江美术学院。中国美术家协会会员。现为中国美术学院教授。

喻慧（女，1960 年生）

江苏南京人。毕业于江苏省国画院。中国美术家协会会员，江苏省美术家协会理事，南京大学艺术研究院特聘教授。现为中国工笔画学会副会长、江苏省国画院副院长、中国国家画院研究员。

陈翔（1963 年生）

上海人。毕业于复旦大学。上海中国画院画师，中国美术家协会会员，上海市美术家协会常务理事。现为上海中国画院副院长。

洪健（1967 年生）

广东潮阳人。毕业于上海大学美术学院。上海中国画院画师，中国美术家协会会员，上海市美术家协会理事。现为上海中国画院展览部副主任。

鲍莺（女，1970 年生）

江苏无锡人。毕业于上海大学美术学院。上海中国画院画师，中国美术家协会会员。

庞飞（1973 年生）

陕西紫阳人。毕业于宝鸡文理学院。上海中国画院画师，中国美术家协会会员。

About the Painters

Chen Peiqiu

Chen Peiqiu was born in 1923 in Nanyang, Henan Province. Chen graduated from the National College of Art in Chongqing. She is a painter at the Shanghai Institute of Chinese Painting and serves as a member of the Shanghai Research Institute of Culture and History, as well as the China Artists Association. She is also an honorary Advisor to the Shanghai Artists Association and an Advisor to the Shanghai Institute of Chinese Painting. Chen also works as an adjunct professor at the College of Fine Arts in Shanghai University. Now she is the President of the Shanghai Institute of Chinese Painting and the Director of Haishang Society of Seal Arts.

Lin Ximing

Lin Ximing was born in 1926 in YongJia, Zhejiang Province. He is a painter at the Shanghai Institute of Chinese Painting, a member of the Shanghai Research Institute of Culture and History and the the China Artists Association, as well as an adjunct professor at the College of Fine Arts in Shanghai University. Lin once served as the Honorary Chairman of the Institute of Chinese Paper-cutting and later the Chairman of it.

Chen Jialing

Chen Jialing was born in 1937 in Hangzhou, Zhejiang Province. Graduating from the Zhejiang Academy of Fine Arts (now China Academy of Art), he is now an adjunct painter at the Shanghai Institute of Chinese Painting, a member of the the China Artists Association, a professor at the College of Fine Arts in Shanghai University, and a researcher at the Chinese National Academy of Painting.

Dai Dunbang

Dai Dunbang, born in 1938, is native to Zhenjiang, Jiangsu Province. Graduating from Shanghai First Normal School, he is now an adjunct painter at the Shanghai Institute of Chinese Painting, a member of the China Artists Association and a professor at Shanghai Jiao Tong University.

Zhang Guiming

Zhang Guiming was born in 1939 inShaoxing, ZhejiangProvince, and passed away in Shanghaiin September 2014. Graduating from Zhejiang Academy of Fine Arts (now China Academy of Art), he is now an adjunct painter at the Shanghai Institute of Chinese Painting, a member of the China Artists Association and a researcher at the China National Academy of Painting. He once served as the Vice President of the Shanghai Institute of Chinese Painting and as the Executive Curator at the LiuHaisuArt Museum.

Yang Zhengxin

Yang Zhengxin was born in 1942 in Shanghai. Graduating from Shanghai Fine Arts School, he is now a painter at the Shanghai Institute of Chinese Painting, a member of the China Artists Association and an adjunct professor at the College of Fine Arts in Shanghai University.

Xiao Haichun

Xiao Haichun was born in 1944 in Fengcheng, Jiangxi Province. Graduating from Shanghai Arts and Crafts College, he now works as an adjunct painter at the Shanghai Institute of Chinese Painting and is a master of arts and crafts. He is also a member of the Shanghai Artists Association.

Cai Tianxiong

Cai Tianxiong was born in 1944 in Wuxi, Jiangsu Province. Graduating from Shanghai Arts and Crafts College, he is now an adjunct painter at the Shanghai Institute of Chinese Painting and a member of the China Artists Association. He once worked as the Director of the Research Office for Traditional Chinese Painting in Shanghai Arts and Crafts College.

Han Shuo

Han Shuo was born in 1945 in Hangzhou, Zhejiang Province. Graduating from the College of Fine Arts in Shanghai University, he is now a painter at the Shanghai Institute of Chinese Painting and an adjunct professor at the College of Fine Arts in Shanghai University. He once served as the Vice President of the Shanghai Institute of Chinese Painting and the council member of the China Artists Association. Han now works as the Director of Art Council of the Shanghai Institute of Chinese Painting and the Vice President of Chinese Painting Institute.

Zhang Leiping

Zhang Leiping was born in 1945 in Yueqing, Zhejiang Province. Graduating from Shanghai Theatre Academy, she is now a painter at the Shanghai Institute of Chinese Painting, a member of the China Artists Association and an Advisor to Shanghai Artists Association. She once served as the Vice Chairman of the Shanghai Artists Association and the Vice President of the Shanghai Institute of Chinese Painting.

Zhang Peicheng

Zhang Peicheng was born in 1948 in Taicang, Jiangsu Province. He is now an adjunct painter at the Shanghai Institute of Chinese Painting, a member of the China Artists Association and an adjunct professor at the College of Fine Arts in Shanghai University. He once served as the Executive Curator at the Liu Haisu Art Museum. Now he is the Vice Chairman of the Shanghai Artists Association.

Lu Fusheng

Lu Fusheng was born in 1949 in Dongyang, Zhejiang Province. Graduating from the Zhejiang Academy of Fine Arts (now China Academy of Art), he is now an adjunct painter at the Shanghai Institute of Chinese Painting and a member of the Shanghai Research Institute of Culture and History. He also serves as the council member of the China Artists Association, the Vice Chairman of the Shanghai Artists Association, an adjunct professor at the China Academy of Art, and the Chief Editor of the Shanghai Literature and Art Publishing House.

Jiang Hong

Jiang Hong was born in 1949 in Shanghai. He is an adjunct painter at the Shanghai Institute of Chinese Painting, and the council member of the Shanghai Artists Association. He once served as the Executive President of the Shanghai Painting and Calligraphy Academy.

Shi Dawei

Shi Dawei was born in 1950 in Huzhou, Zhejiang Province. Graduating from the College of Fine Arts in Shanghai University, he is now an adjunct professor at this college. He is a member of the National Committee of Chinese People's Political Consultative Conference. He also serves as the Vice Chairman of the China Artists Association, the Chairman of the Shanghai Federation of Literary and Art Circles, as well as the Shanghai Artists Association. He is a member of and a researcher at the China National Academy of Painting, the Curator of the China Art Museum and the President of the Shanghai Institute of Chinese Painting.

Che Pengfei

Che Pengfei was born in 1951 in Laiyang, Shandong Province, and a graduate of Shanghai Normal University. As the former Vice-President of the Shanghai Institute of Chinese Painting, he is now a painter at the Shanghai Institute of Chinese Painting, a member of the China Artists Association, and Executive member of the council of Shanghai Artists Association.

Zhu Xinchang

Zhu Xinchang was born in 1954 in Ningbo, Zhejiang Province, and graduated from the Shanghai Normal University. He is now a painter at the Shanghai Institute of Chinese Painting, a member of the China Artists Association, and the council member of the Shanghai Artists Association.

Ma Xiaojuan

Ma Xiaojuan was born in 1955 in Nanjing, Jiangsu Province. Graduating from China Academy of Art, she now works as a painter at the Shanghai Institute of Chinese Painting, a member of the China Artists Association, Executive member of the council of Shanghai Artists Association, and Director of Teaching and Research Office of the Shanghai Institute of Chinese Painting.

Gao Yun

Gao Yun was born in 1956 in Nanjing, Jiangsu Province. Graduating from Nanjing Arts University, he is now a member of the National Committee of Chinese People's Political Consultative Conference. He serves as the Vice Director of the Traditional Chinese Painting Council of the China Artists Association, the Vice President of the Chinese Painting Institute, the Vice Director of the Committee of Art Museums in China. He is also a member of and a researcher at the China National Academy of Painting, a researcher on Chinese paintings at the Graduate School of Chinese National Academy of Arts, an honorary Curator at the Jiangsu Art Museum, and the Deputy Director of Jiangsu Provincial Department of Culture.

Chen Xiangxun

Chen Xiangxun was born in 1956 in Hangzhou, Zhejiang Province, and graduated from the Zhejiang Academy of Fine Arts (now China Academy of Art). As the former Dean of the Traditional Chinese Painting Department of the China Academy of Art, he is now a member of the China Artists Association. He serves at the Academic Committee and works as a professor at the Traditional Chinese Painting Department of the China Academy of Art, and he is also a researcher at the China National Academy of Painting.

Zhu Min

Zhu Min was born in 1956 in Xinchang, Zhejiang Province. Graduating from Zhejiang Academy of Fine Arts (now China Academy of Art), he is now a painter at the Shanghai Institute of Chinese Painting, the council member of the Shanghai Artists Association, and the Vice Director of the Research and Production Office of the Shanghai Institute of Chinese Painting.

Le Zhenwen

Le Zhenwen was born in 1956 in Zhenhai, Zhejiang Province. Once worked as the Dean of the Traditional Chinese Painting Department at the College of Fine Arts in Shanghai University, he is now an adjunct painter at the Shanghai Institute of Chinese Painting, a member of the China Artists Association, the council member of the Shanghai Artists Association, the President of the Xu Beihong Art School of Shanghai Maritime University, and the Executive President of the Shanghai Painting and Calligraphy Academy.

Ding Xiaofang

Ding Xiaofang was born in 1957 in Shaoxing, Zhejiang Province. Graduating from the College of Fine Arts in Shanghai University, he is now a painter at the Shanghai Institute of Chinese Painting, a member of the China Artists Association, and the council member of the Shanghai Artists Association.

Wang Jiafang

Wang Jiafang was born in 1959 in Jiading, Shanghai Municipality. Graduating from East China Normal University, Wang is now an adjunct painter at the Shanghai Institute of Chinese Painting, a member of the China Artists Association, and the Executive council member of the Shanghai Artists Association.

He Xi

He Xi was born in 1960 in Jiaxing, Zhejiang Province. Graduating from Zhejiang Academy of Fine Arts (now China Academy of Art), he is now a painter at the Shanghai Institute of Chinese Painting, a member of the China Artists Association, a council member of the Shanghai Artists Association, and the Director of Creativity and Research Office of the Shanghai Institute of Chinese Painting.

Xu Mo

Xu Mo was born in 1960 in Fuzhou, Fujian Province. Graduating from Zhejiang Academy of Fine Arts (now China Academy of Art), he is now a member of the China Artists Association, and a professor at the China Academy of Art.

Yu Hui

Yu Hui was born in 1960 in Nanjing, Jiangsu Province. Graduating from Jiangsu Traditional Chinese Painting Institute, she is now a member of the China Artists Association, council member of the Jiangsu Artists Association, and a distinguished Professor at the Academy of Arts in Nanjing University. She now serves as the Vice President of the China HUE Art Society, the Vice President of the Jiangsu Traditional Chinese Painting Institute, and a researcher at the China National Academy of Painting.

Chen Xiang

Chen Xiang was born in 1963 in Shanghai. Graduating from Fudan University, he is now a painter at the Shanghai Institute of Chinese Painting, a member of the China Artists Association, an Executive member of the council of the Shanghai Artists Association, and the Vice President of the Shanghai Institute of Chinese Painting.

Hong Jian

Hong Jian was born in 1967 in Chaoyang, Guangdong Province. Graduating from the College of Fine Arts in Shanghai University, he is now a painter at the Shanghai Institute of Chinese Painting, a member of the China Artists Association, council member of the Shanghai Artists Association, and the Vice Director of the Department of Exhibition of the Shanghai Institute of Chinese Painting.

Bao Ying

Bao Ying was born in 1970 in Wuxi, Jiangsu Province. Graduating from the College of Fine Arts in Shanghai University, she is now a painter at the Shanghai Institute of Chinese Painting and a member of the China Artists Association.

Pang Fei

Pang Fei was born in 1973 in Ziyang, Shaanxi Province. Graduating from Baoji University of Arts and Sciences, he is now a painter at the Shanghai Institute of Chinese Painting and a member of the China Artists Association.

译者简介

许渊冲（1921 年生）

北京大学教授，是唯一一位将中国诗词译成英法韵文多达一百余部的著名翻译家。中文著作有《翻译的艺术》《文学翻译谈》等；英文著作有《中诗英韵探胜——从诗经到西厢记》《逝水年华》等。英文译著有《诗经》《楚辞》《论语》《老子》《唐诗三百首》《宋词三百首》《元曲三百首》《西厢记》等。法文译著有《中国古诗词三百首》《诗经选》《唐诗选》《宋词选》等。中文译著有英国桂冠诗人德莱顿的诗剧、司各特的小说、法国作家雨果的《艾那尼》、司汤达的《红与黑》、巴尔扎克的《高老头》、福楼拜的《包法利夫人》、罗曼·罗兰的《约翰·克里斯托夫》等。1999 年被提名为诺贝尔文学奖候选人。2010 年获得中国翻译协会用于表彰个人的最高荣誉奖项“中国翻译文化终身成就奖”。2014 年获得国际翻译界最高奖项之一——国际翻译家联盟（国际译联）2014“北极光”杰出文学翻译奖。

About the Translator

Xu Yuanchong (1921–)

Professor at Peking University, author and / or translator of 120 literary works in Chinese, English and / or French. His writings in Chinese and / or English include *Art of Translation*, *On Literary Translation*, *On Chinese Verse in English Rhyme from the Book of Poetry to the Romance of the Western Bower*, *Vanished Springs*, etc. His English translations include *Book of Poetry*, *Elegies of the South*, *Thus Spoke the Master*, *Laws Divine and Human*, *300 Tang Poems*, *300 Song Lyrics*, *300 Yuan Songs*, *Romance of the Western Bower*, etc. His French translations include *300 Poèmes Chinois Classiques*, etc. His translations from English and French authors include Dryden's *All For Love*, Scott's *Quentin Durward* , Hugo's *Hernani*, Stendhal's *Le Rouge et le Noir*, Balzac's *Le Père Goriot*, Flaubert's *Madame Bovary*, Roman Rolland's *Jean Christophe*, etc. In 1999, he was nominated as a candidate for the Nobel Prize in Literature. In 2010, he received from the Translations Association of China (TAC) "Translation and Culture Lifetime Achievement Award", the highest honorary award for a Chinese translator. In 2014, he won the Federation of International Translators (FIT) "Aurora Borealis" Prize for Outstanding Translation of Fiction Literature, one of the highest prizes in the international translation world.

图书在版编目(CIP)数据

画说宋词：汉英对照／许渊冲译；陈佩秋等绘．
—北京：中译出版社，2017.11（2019.3重印）
ISBN 978-7-5001-5437-2

Ⅰ.①画… Ⅱ.①许… ②陈… Ⅲ.①宋词—选集
—汉、英②中国画—作品集—中国—现代
Ⅳ. ①I222.844②J222.7

中国版本图书馆CIP数据核字(2017)第244170号

出版发行／中译出版社
地　　址／北京市西城区车公庄大街甲4号物华大厦6层
电　　话／(010) 68359376，68359303（发行部）68359719（编辑部）
邮　　编／100044
传　　真／(010) 68357870
电子邮箱／book@ctph.com.cn
网　　址／http://www.ctph.com.cn

策　　划／许　琳　费滨海　鲍炳新
出 品 人／张高里　贾兵伟
中文审订／孙曼均
英文审订／章婉凝
责任编辑／刘香玲
装帧设计／张培成　单　勇　胡小慧
印　　刷／山东临沂新华印刷物流集团有限责任公司

规　　格／787mm×1092mm　1/16
印　　张／23
字　　数／210千字
版　　次／2017年11月第1版
印　　次／2019年3月第3次

ISBN 978-7-5001-5437-2　定价：96.00元

中　译　出　版　社